Rasputin's Scorn

Rasputin's Dynasty Trilogy

Courtnee Turner Hoyle

Courtnee Turner Hoyle

Rasputin's Scorn

Rasputin's Dynasty Trilogy

Copyright © June 1, 2022

Erwin, Tennessee

by Courtnee Turner Hoyle

Library of Congress Control Number: 2022907481

Print IBSN 979-8-9855408-2-6

Electronic IBSN 979-8-9855408-3-3

This book is a work of fiction. Names, characters, businesses, places, events, and incidents are the product of the author's imagination or used in a fictitious manner. Any similarities or resemblance to actual persons, living or dead, events, or places is entirely coincidental.

Cover Design: Sweet15 Designs, LLC

Author Photo: Tosha Cannon

Contents

To Stereling and Legacee,
the reflection of Razz and Lexi
Both of you are *rich kids*.

Rasputin's Scorn Playlist

1. "Don't Tread on Me" Metallica
2. "Burning Bright" Shinedown
3. "Rich Kids" New Medicine*
4. "Right Above It" Lil' Wayne (featuring Drake)*
5. "Where'd You Go?" Fort Minor (featuring Holly Brook and Jonah Matranga)*
6. "Shots" Imagine Dragons*
7. "Cupid's Chokehold" Gym Class Heroes
8. "Drown" Bring Me the Horizon
9. "Stressed Out" Twenty-One Pilots
10. "Hall of Fame" The Script (featuring will.i.am)
11. "Chicken Dance" Werner Thomas
12. "Cecelia and the Satellite" Andrew McMahon in the Wilderness
13. "Hollow Moon (Bad Wolf)" AWOL Nation*
14. "New Divide" Linkin Park
15. "Other Side" Ozzy Osbourne
16. "My Blood" Twenty-One Pilots

*Some explicit lyrics

CHAPTER ONE

Blood marched through my brain, and my skin shivered with electricity. The possibility of holding Scorn in my hand was within my reach.

Thousands of tiny vials of the powder mocked me from ten feet away. I was so close that I could smell their rusty aroma.

Two men dressed in black leather talked in unintelligible whispers. They gestured occasionally, oblivious to my presence in the direction they pointed.

The wind knocked the moonlit window I had left open. It banged against the stillness, drawing the attention of the guards.

I slipped down the pole carefully and hid behind it. My body spilled out from each side, but I was dressed in black jeans and a shirt, and the shadows concealed me.

The men moved in my direction. I tried to remember the Tai-Kaun-Do class I took in fifth grade, and I wondered if my thirty minutes in martial arts would save me.

An accented voice carried against the cool walls. A figure that commanded all our attention stepped into view. I only saw the outline of the stranger, but I could feel the power that radiated from his presence. The men's posture straightened, and they awaited instructions. The voice spoke to them in another language, and the men abruptly complied.

I held my position, hardly breathing. I'd be dead if the men discovered me, possibly worse. My legs wanted to run, but my brain told my body to remain in place. Moments stretched through time while I waited for the dark figure to leave. Sweat rolled down my face and back, and my heart was beating so loudly, that I was convinced I could hear it echo against the walls of my chest.

His footsteps pounded against the concrete and reverberated through my feet. He stopped at the bin that held the vials of Scorn, and he scooped up a handful. He plucked up one thoughtfully, holding it against the trickle of moonlight.

I felt, more than saw, his eyes dart briefly to my position. I wanted to bolt down the hall, but I remained in place, not even chancing a breath.

He tossed the vial onto the floor casually, as if he were doing nothing more than dusting a crumb from his cloak. The vessel landed several feet from my position, but it was still a great risk to grab it. It would mean full exposure on the cameras. The men who guarded the facility may not know my exact features, other than accurate guesses about my height and weight, but they would be aware that someone was here and had picked up the vial.

Was the man testing me? I had heard reports that Scorn made people desperate for the pinch in their nerves and the bite in their muscles as their body stretched past normal physical limits. There had been rumors about people selling a family member for one vial.

Was he trying to root me out of my spot so that he could call the guards to grab me? I decided against it. Something told me that the man could easily dispatch me.

Was he offering me a taste of his product so that I could become one of the millions of addicts worldwide? A vial that small would only last a short time, and Scorn users needed a steady supply for the rest of their lives.

I stayed rooted to my spot and waited for him to allude to my presence or say something in my direction.

Surrounded by darkness, the man held onto his mystery. He walked away resolutely, betraying a slight limp. The shadows swallowed him and left me to decide my destiny in the stillness of the moonlight.

CHAPTER TWO

I ran through the streets, gripping the vial desperately, convinced that one of the men I had seen would step out of a bush or from behind a house and grab me. I darted through the shadows and dodged the lights. My dark hair fell between my glasses and my eyes, obscuring my view. It had grown longer over the past few months, but my mom hadn't been able to cut it.

The running water in the creek muffled the sounds of my feet. It was almost spring, and a recent flash flood had caused the water to lick the top of the banks. I ducked between the houses and surveyed my open bedroom window from behind a tree. When I was certain no one was watching, I hopped into my room, hardly fluttering the curtain.

I had made it. The vial rested in my hand, heavier with meaning than weight.

I stared at the sticker on the clear plastic vial. An ouroboros, or a black snake eating its own tail, trademarked the drug and its street value. In ancient Egyptian and Greek cultures, the ouroboros signified infinity, and most people thought the drug gave the user an "infinite" amount of power, like an immortal. The insignia showed up on every national and local news program when they sought to report about the effect Scorn had on the people who took it.

No one would ever understand what I had done to get the container. Its contents were no more than a couple of ounces, but it was the key to escape from my circumstances.

I had been given the same anti-drug speeches as my classmates, and I knew the effects of taking drugs. I'd never consider taking any other drug. They were all less than appealing to me, but Scorn was different. The tiny amount in my possession could hold my family together, even if my mom was dying.

I slipped into the hall and confirmed my mom's steady breathing. She hadn't caught me.

I wriggled out of my clothes and bounced lightly on the bed. I doubted that my pounding adrenalin would allow me to sleep, but I was going to pretend to rest.

"Razzberry," my mom called.

The nickname wouldn't have been received well if someone else had said it. She had created it so that she wouldn't have to call me the name my dad had given me.

I put on a pair of sleep shorts and hurried to my mom's room. I could smell death just outside the door, lurking in wait.

I poured my mom another glass of water from the pitcher and sat on the end of the bed. The disease had not marked her beauty yet. Her light hair pulled the moonlight from the window, her lips were full, and her almond eyes were sharp.

"How long were you gone tonight?" she asked.

I started to deny it, but she held up her hand. "I can smell rain on you," she declared.

I nodded, but I didn't commit to anything.

My mother smiled serenely. "Who is the lucky person?"

She had rattled me, but I tried not to let it show. I said the first name that popped into my mind. "Loila."

"Is that the little blonde girl who thought she was a unicorn?" she mused.

I rolled my eyes. "That was in third grade, Mom."

"I liked her, Razzberry," she quietly defended. "Does she still have an unhealthy obsession with mythical creatures?"

I stared at my hands and concentrated on putting one finger over the next one. I didn't know how to answer her, and I wanted to go back to my bed, where I could think about the contents of the vial.

"I'm only joking," my mom laughed, pulling a freezing hand from her blanket and placing it over my fingers. "I trust your judgement."

She stared up at the ceiling and a smile touched her lips. "Your father and I used to sneak away from time to time."

It had been six years, but my dad's death still seemed unreal. He would have fit so perfectly in my world, and he could have helped us find better medical treatment for my mom, but part of me still resented him for the way he left.

"He certainly knew how to sneak off," I commented.

"That's not fair," my mother scolded. "He must have had his reasons."

"Yeah," I mocked. "Leave his family for fame and glory."

"It's been years, Razzberry. If he left a legacy, it's been forgotten."

I could feel the tension from my mom's shaky breaths. I remembered her sickness and shifted the conversation to a more agreeable point.

"Monique will be mad at me if I keep you up all night."

"I guess we should get some sleep," she agreed. "I'm introducing nouns tomorrow."

I had been part of my mom's lesson plans periodically. "Is this the one where they run around the room with a label machine?"

"Yes," she nodded. "It promises to be an active day, but I'll have an assistant with me."

I patted my mom's leg and hugged her.

"No more trips out to see Loila tonight," my mom said.

"No," I chuckled. "I'm in for the night."

Back in my room, my hand gripped the vial, and if I stared at it long enough, the snake seemed to move, as if it were devouring itself on an endless loop. A tiny packet of rust-colored powder slid easily around its plastic confines. I tucked it into the pocket of my sleep shorts and settled into bed. The contents could provide an escape from the reality of a world where my mom was dying.

Adrenaline had completed its cycle through my body, and I was able to relax. I stared out at the moon between my blinds and blinked in the white light. Tomorrow would mark a new day. One where I had more control.

CHAPTER THREE

Monique burst through my door, commanding my attention. I rubbed my eyes, uncertain of the time.

"Will you talk some sense into her?" she demanded.

I nodded agreeably, but I made no attempt to move. Before I could protest, Monique dragged me down the hall to the kitchen.

"Tell him," she barked at my mom.

"Tell him what?" my mom defended haughtily. "I am an adult. I can make my own decisions."

"Sure," Monique agreed, "but your decisions affect the other people in your life."

My mom busied herself with Monique's coffee. Her deliberate movements indicated her level of stress was way above normal range.

"What is it?" I asked. I still wasn't awake enough to handle a serious conversation.

Monique put her hand on her hip. "Your mother has decided that she's not going to continue her treatment."

My mom's defeated posture was the only confirmation I needed. She turned around and addressed us. "I don't want to spend my final days feeling crappy and walking around in a haze. It's better to have quality time than a quantity of time."

"What about Lexi?" I said.

As if on cue, Lexi hopped across the floor and dropped into her chair. "Good morning," she spoke, not sensing the tension.

"Good morning," our mom returned, pushing a bowl of fruit to her daughter.

Monique continued to stand behind me, and I was very aware of my clothes, or lack of them. I had known Monique for most of my life, or all of it that I could remember, but I didn't like anyone to see me with my shirt off except for my mom and sister.

"You guys are weird," Lexi observed, after she noticed us staring at her. She whipped her blond hair to the side when it almost fell into her fruit.

"Nothing escapes the attention of an eight-year-old," my mom sighed.

"We'll talk about this later," Monique promised, releasing her hold on my arm.

I jogged back to my room, and I pulled out the powder in my pocket. It seemed like a good time to use it, especially after what I had heard in the kitchen.

I showered and expelled a fog of body spray in my room. I listened to my sister whine about ecology homework as I watched the mist settle onto my clothes. To an outside observer, my sister might appear too young to study the way plants and animals react in a chosen environment, but my sister was convinced she could prevent deforestation by mentioning it every day.

I loved my family but interacting with them was draining. My sister was a little too wild, even without sugar, and Monique continuously tried to engage me in conversation. I would have been perfectly content with eating a bowl of cereal without Lexi in my lap while I tried to dodge Monique's questions about my last science experiment.

To be fair, it was part of her job. She worked with my mom at the school, but she taught eighth grade science, and my mom educated first graders. My mom had prepared me for Pale Woods Academy from a young age, so it was no surprise when my above-average test scores guaranteed a scholarship to the school. The endowment extended to my sister, even though her scores were lower than mine. Monique couldn't help my sister in reading, but she tasked herself with the responsibility of making sure that my sister and I remained ahead of our peers in science.

"Razzberry," my mom called. "It's time to go."

My sister and I dutifully lined up in the hall. Our mom kissed each of us, and Lexi followed Monique to the door while I dug in my pockets for my house key.

Monique took us to school every morning so my mom could meditate. We used to relax with her, but Lexi was too fidgety.

My mom's bedroom door clicked behind me as I walked down the hall. My sister and Monique were waiting on me in the living room.

"I don't like her," Lexi told Monique.

"You may not want to let her know it, though," Monique counseled. "Her father owns Bounce Time, and her friends get in for free."

Lexi's nose went up. "I don't need to get into Bounce Time for free," she said proudly. "I have my own money."

"Suit yourself," Monique returned. "But rich people can open a lot of doors."

"I can do that myself, too," my sister quipped, and demonstrated her ability by opening the back door.

Monique sighed, and breezed into the cool, gray morning.

CHAPTER FOUR

The cheerleaders buzzed around the flyers for the upcoming banquet. Pale Woods Academy held sections for students from ages five to eighteen, so the information about the eighth grade banquet was sandwiched between a prom announcement and the poster for the kindergartener's spring recital.

Kelly, the cheer captain, spoke loudly about the elaborate dress she had chosen. My eyes settled on her, even though I didn't care about the topic. She was voluptuous and symmetrical, so it was easy to stare at her without realizing it.

Loila rattled my locker. "Hey."

"Hey," I returned, in a tone I hoped was smooth.

"Tabitha wants me to try out for cheerleading," she said.

I nodded. It was hard to tell if Loila wanted me to be for or against the idea.

"Do I look like a cheerleader?" she asked me.

There it was: the loaded question. *What was I supposed to say?* If I said yes, then she might get mad if she thought that I was comparing her to all the cheerleader stereotypes. Loila was smart and caring. She wasn't the type of girl who laughed at other girls in glasses or refused access to her table at lunch. On the other hand, if I said no, then she might think that I believed she wasn't pretty enough.

I settled on the most neutral response. "I don't know."

Thankfully, it was the right answer.

Loila's chocolate eyes revealed nothing until she said, "I don't know either."

I tried not to make my relief visible. I took her library books and carried them in my other hand until we passed the library and she asked me to push them through the drop. Since our books were on tablets, it was the most chivalrous thing I could do.

"What if people think I'm just eye candy with no thoughts on current issues because I joined the team?" she worried.

"Then they don't know you."

Loila half-smiled, and one of her dimples winked at me. I stared at my feet to keep from looking at her too long.

"I know I can keep up with the routines," she went on. "I've taken dance classes for years. I just don't want to be looked at the wrong way."

"You could be the one that changes the stereotype," I suggested.

"Sure," Loila said, but she didn't seem convinced.

Mr. Fritz had already started the class when we sat down. He glanced at Loila and me irritably, but he didn't stop the lecture to reprimand us.

I tried to stay awake, but the events leading up to World War One were dry and confusing. My eyes lolled in their sockets until someone's tablet slid off their desk and slammed onto the floor.

I tried to remember the boy's name and decided I didn't care. I liked most of the kids in my classes but very few of them were memorable. They were just blurs in a sea of faces I navigated around every school year.

Mr. Fritz eyed the owner of the tablet until it was clear that it wasn't intentional. The boy who had accidentally eased it off his desk slouched, painfully aware of all the eyes on him.

"Tsar Nicholas II faced assassination because of his decision to stay in the war," he lectured. "His family and those close to him were in mortal peril, as well."

Sara raised her hand. "I watched the movie about that," she informed us.

"Oh, really," Mr. Fritz returned, impressed. "Which one?"

"Anastasia."

The class chuckled. Mr. Fritz hushed them, but he turned around to keep a smile off his lips.

"That's the movie where Rasputin killed the whole family," a guy from the back of the room said.

Mr. Fritz could feel the tone of his lecture moving in a less than intellectual direction. That's not historically accurate," he interjected.

"Yeah, and then he tried to kill Anastasia when she remembered who she was," another voice piped up.

"Actually," I told them, "Rasputin was a mystic. He helped Alexi, the Tsar's youngest son, before the Romanov family was assassinated."

The class was shocked that I had spoken. The kids that had been in other classes with me knew that I was smart, but I usually didn't speak up in class.

"He's the man they couldn't kill," an overly exuberant boy stated. He mimicked machine gun fire. "They had to shot him and throw him into a river."

"They tried to poison him first," Loila remarked. "But it didn't work. He was shot a couple of times before he died."

"What if he didn't die?" Sara spoke eerily.

"They found his body," Loila confirmed. "There's a picture of him with a gunshot wound through his head."

The boy rocked from imaginary bullets again. He fell onto the floor, kicking his legs.

Mr. Fritz tried to control the class before it got away from him. "That's enough. Rasputin was a mysterious figure, but he doesn't play a large role in our lesson."

"That's debatable," I said, collecting everyone's attention again. "Alexi was a hemophiliac, and after he healed him a couple of times, Rasputin had some influence over the Tsar and Tsarina."

"What's a hemo-pli-ac," the boy in front of me said.

"It's when you bleed freely," Mr. Fritz answered. "Now, we need to get back to the actual lesson."

"Did they kill Rasputin's family too?" Loila's friend, Tabitha, asked.

"No," I answered. "The imperial family protected them."

"Or they had mysterious powers like their father," another girl hinted.

"No, I think one of his children died of dysentery," I commented. "No magical powers there."

"Maybe Rasputin and the tsarina had a child," Sara speculated.

Loila looked at me and rolled her eyes before she addressed her. "Rasputin had a mistress, but it wasn't the tsarina."

Mr. Fritz held up his hands. "Okay, okay. I like all this talk about a historical figure, but could we get back to the lesson?"

The bell rang, and the class dismissed his words with the roar of chairs scraping against the tiles. I closed my book with a pop, happy that no one had thought to link my name with the mysterious Grigori Rasputin.

CHAPTER FIVE

Aiden met me at the door, and we fist bumped. We had been friends since the first grade, and by some fortunate turn of events that may or may not have been due to my mom's influence over the middle-aged man responsible for student schedules, we had been placed in all the same classes.

"Dude, you know a lot about Rasputin," he gaped. He was fishing for a part of me that I usually kept tucked neatly away in a compartment with restricted access.

"My dad used to talk about him."

The mention of my father caused anyone to clam up. They didn't want to upset me, and my comments about him usually made people uncomfortable.

"I heard Loila's gonna try out for cheerleading," he laughed, changing the subject. "Does that mean you're going to be the school's new quarterback?"

I was tall and toned, but I wasn't close to football material. His joke had more to do with the unspoken social status in our school.

"Loila will make it," I told him.

"Yeah, I know," he responded more seriously. "I'm actually kinda worried about her."

I nodded my head. I felt the same way, but I didn't commit to it by saying anything about the way I felt.

"Have you heard about the Rituals?"

Everyone at the school knew about the Rituals the athletic kids had to go through to be accepted. You made the team at tryouts, but you didn't really belong to it until you passed the tasks they set out for you. My mom called it hazing, and she persuaded me not to join a sports team. The teachers knew about it, and their silence encouraged it.

At first, it seemed innocent. The older members of the team would tell a new football player to give himself a mohawk or pierce his nose. The other players wanted their classmates to see their influence on a gullible student. But then, the poor kid would have to do something scary to prove his worth, like go in a haunted house or spend the night in Pale Woods.

The cheerleading teams had to find unique ways to cover up their Rituals. Their coach had gone to school at Pale Woods Academy, and she wouldn't allow the Rituals to be a rite of passage on her squad. The cheerleaders found a way to haze their new girls, though. It was easier for the group that moved from elementary school to sixth grade, as they could go through their hazing together, but anyone who joined in seventh or eighth grades had to go through their tasks alone.

I stared at Aiden, and he took it as his cue to continue. "I remember hearing about this one girl a long time ago. One of the cheerleaders had her older brother lead the girl to Lost Cove. She had to spend the night in an old house."

Lost Cove was an area just inside North Carolina. From my home in Erwin, I could follow the railroad tracks, cross the Tennessee state line, and cut up a hill to the property. My dad had taken me camping and hiking in the area when I was young. Only one house and a graveyard still stood in the forgotten town. The people had walked away from their homes when the Clinchfield Railroad ceased stopping with supplies for their small community. It was an isolated place, and I had loved hiding in an abandoned rusted truck and picking huge blueberries.

I let him ramble on about the girl, but I knew the story. The girl had been Mae Gable, a thirteen-year-old girl with big plans to enter the fashion industry.

Some of the cheerleaders had hiked back with the brother the next morning to pick up Mae, but they couldn't find her. They searched the old ghost town, but there was no sign of her. Finally, they decided that she had gotten scared and ran into the surrounding woods. They had searched for her for hours, scared of getting into trouble, but they finally had to call the police.

Search parties combed the area for weeks. Her parents and her sister never gave up hope, but the townspeople assumed that she had been picked up by a hiker, eaten by a wild animal, or wandered into a cave.

Finally, a team of young men decided to investigate the buildings in Lost Cove again. They found her underneath one of the old houses.

"They said her face was frozen in silent horror," Aiden quoted from the most infamous local documentary about the event. He mimicked the open-mouth stare of certain death.

I punched him on his arm. "Not cool, man."

Aiden rubbed his arm and chuckled. "Seriously, though. I don't want to see someone like Loila have to go through The Rituals."

"Yeah," I agreed.

"You boys are going to be late for class."

We had stopped outside the room next to our second period class. The teacher, Mrs. Holt, had poked her head out of the door to move us along. Her coaches whistle dangled within view.

I smiled at her. "Yes, ma'am," I returned agreeably.

She ducked her head back into her room. The class joined her in a meticulous recitation of the preamble of the American Constitution.

"I'm glad Mr. Fritz doesn't make us do that," Aiden remarked.

Monique was waiting at the door for us with a stack of papers in her hand. I didn't pretend that I had forgotten the quiz. She would have known it was a lie.

I had to call Monique "Mr. Sams" at school. She was untraditional, and she wanted the students to address her by her first name, but the school insisted that a title precede her surname. She applied their rule technically. At first, students were confused by it, but they understood the reason for it after they met Monique. She rebelled against most of our town's easily accepted social conventions. Three dogs, five cats, and a bearded lizard lived in her house, she'd never learned to cook—even though the townspeople kept reminding her that it was a skill that was necessary for a good marriage—and she mowed her grass on Sunday, if she bothered to mow it at all.

"Cool ink bottle," Aiden said about the tattoo on her forearm.

At first, she didn't know what he meant, and she followed his gaze. "That's actually a bottle of poison."

My mom had hinted that Monique had lived a different life before they became friends. After witnessing her pale, skeletal features turn more robust and rosier, I decided that she had been on drugs. I questioned my mom about it, but she only made vague references to Monique's past, unwilling to betray her friend. I wondered if the tattoo was a mark from the time before she knew us.

We took the empty seats at the front of the classroom and started the quiz. Most kids in eighth grade learned a small section on genetics and DNA, but it was Monique's favorite subject.

"Remember," she reminded us, as she passed out the papers, "G-enomes tell you the potential of your DNA. It's the combined sum of both of your parents. But phenomes are your actual attributes." She stopped when most of the class stared at her with open mouths. "Well, I guess we'll see how you guys do on the quiz."

The quiz was supposed to assess what we already knew so that she could build her lectures to fill in the parts where the class was deficient, and it seemed like Monique would be reteaching us what she considered to be foundational genetic concepts.

I finished the quiz quickly, and I closed my eyes while the rest of the class struggled to complete the work. Monique talked about genetics frequently, so the Pungent Squares had been easy for me.

People coughed, chairs shifted, birds chirped. It all culminated into a background symphony.

Monique announced the end of the quiz and took up the remaining papers. We watched a video about genetic sequencing for the rest of the class time while she huffed over the quizzes she evaluated. The class must have been woefully ignorant about genetics.

We had lunch after our second period class, and Aiden filled his tray with various fruits from a large buffet bowl. As he added two extra chocolate milks to his lunch, he caught me looking at his pile of strawberries and grapes.

"What?" he asked, plucking a grape from its stem. "It's healthy."

"And expensive," I added.

Aiden shrugged his shoulders. The school allowed the students an individual fruit or a handful of smaller fruits. Additional fruit was added to our lunch total.

The lunch lady looked down her nose at Aiden when she announced his total. It was the same amount as a week of school lunches, but Aiden swiped his school card like the amount didn't bother him.

I wondered what it was like to be able to afford nice things and extra fruit. Aiden's style was polished, from his spotless white sneakers to his perfectly sculpted hair that rose in spikes along the side of his head. He wore designer clothes, but he never wore shorts.

I saw him change socks once on a field trip. We had been on a hike, and it had started raining. The teacher had cautioned us to bring extra clothes. We were all soaked, and we were ushered into the locker rooms before we boarded the bus. Aiden hadn't changed clothes in front of the other guys, but he put on clean socks. I was closest to him when the leg of his pant raised just enough to show a pink burn just above his ankle. I stayed close to Aiden from that day on. I wanted to be there for him in case he ever wanted to put the person in jail who had placed those marks on his legs.

"Do you want some of this?" Aiden offered when we sat down. "I think I got too much."

Aiden was generous, and he knew that my family struggled. He had paid for my lunch once, and I had almost fought him over it. He understood that the best way for him to give me things was for him to buy an excess and offer it to me.

He dropped a couple of handfuls of fruit on my tray and slid a chocolate milk between us. I filled my belly with my pride intact.

I thought about telling him about the package I had stuffed between my mattresses. I had put the vial in a manilla envelope and moved it there so I wouldn't get caught with it at school. *Would Aiden understand my reasons?*

I spotted Loila across the lunchroom. The artificial light reflected off her hair, and her laugh was like music. I was caught up in its melody when Aiden shook me.

"Dude, when are you going to tell her?"

I was starring right at Loila, so there was no sense pretending like I didn't know who he meant. "We're just friends."

"Whatever," he replied.

I breezed through the rest of the day. When I came into my mom's classroom, it was still buzzing with busy first graders. I helped them pack up and started picking up the trash in the room. When I looked up, my mom was staring at me.

"You're a good son, Razz," she whispered. Tears threatened, but she dismissed them.

My mom had gotten more sentimental since she had been diagnosed. She hugged my sister and me more, and we fought over boundaries and trivial matters less.

"I got an A," my sister announced. She stood at the door, awaiting accolades. My mom and I showered her with praise.

Lexi had been struggling in social studies all school year, but the introduction of the Egyptian civilization had piqued her interests. At first, she had struggled through large texts to enrich the knowledge she shared with her class, but then my mom and I started reading the material to her. Lexi had devoured every morsel of knowledge, and we were excited to see an interest in reading, until she received a low grade on a quiz.

Lexi had been devastated. I had looked over the test, and it covered easy concepts about the Egyptian civilization. I read the questions to Lexi, and she knew the answers. My mom was concerned. She had spoken to a friend at the academy, and her friend loosely evaluated my sister.

She had reported back to my mom that she thought Lexi showed signs of dyslexia. My mom had asked for Lexi to have an IEP, or individualized education plan, added to Lexi's file. It had a lot of educational and legal language in it, but it gave my sister extra time on reading activities, and she sat at a computer that read her tests to her. Lexi had just gotten the results of the first test she had taken since the IEP had been applied.

"My second-grade super star!" our mom beamed.

Lexi pressed the paper into her hand, and my mom surveyed it. My sister pointed to the essay question. Two proud sentences told her feelings about mummification.

"Between your interest in Egypt, and Razz's lecture this morning, our family looks like historians," our mom grinned. "And to think, it was never my favorite subject."

"How did you know about what I said in history class?" I demanded.

My mom placed a gentle hand on my knee. "Teachers talk. You added to the disruption in his lecture, but Mr. Fritz was impressed by your knowledge."

"Was it about Egypt?" my sister inquired, jumping up and down.

There was an uncomfortable pause. Neither my mom nor I wanted to tell my sister the subject of the discussion during my morning history class, but her expectant eyes demanded an answer.

"He talked about Rasputin," my mom said, the tone of her voice dipping.

"Oh," my sister responded flatly.

"I hope he doesn't expect me to carry his class every day," I joked. To my relief, my jibe broke the tension.

"No one would expect too much from a man of few words," my mom teased back.

Lexi turned the light off and on several times. "Let's go," she whined. "I don't like to be at school *all* day."

My mom sighed. She would never have let me act so impatiently, but she didn't want my sister to think of her negatively in the short time she had left with her.

I followed my mom and sister into the hallway. My fragile family was all I had left, and I would do anything to preserve it.

CHAPTER SIX

My mom and I disagreed a lot. We had settled most of our differences since she was diagnosed with a terminal disease, but one thing still caused an uproar in our house: dinner.

My mom decided to be a vegetarian, and she wanted my sister and I to join her choice. My sister was picky about everything, so she didn't mind the switch; it was one less thing on her plate that she'd refuse to finish. On the other hand, I had always had meat with my meals, so it was a little harder for me to let go of it.

My mom tried to compensate for the change by adding meatless substitutes to our meals, but they fell flat. I didn't want to eat plant nuggets and tofu turkey.

I tried to get used to it, but I couldn't eat a lot of the new concoctions. My hunger added to my feelings, and my mom and I exchanged heated words about her meals.

I tried to eat whatever she placed in front of me, but my mom watched me chew, and I felt like she expected me to critique her cooking. Sometimes, I genuinely liked our meals. Soup beans and corn bread was okay, and taco soup had been a hit, but I couldn't eat limited meals forever.

I had a food stash in my room. Beef jerky was usually in it, and Aiden swiped me some cans of tuna from his family's pantry.

My mom tapped her foot in front of the stove, staring at a recipe on her phone. "Do you think I could pull off chicken and dumplings?"

"Sure," I said. "With real chicken."

My mom sighed. She had a grand vision of tofu pieces surrounded by dough and gravy, and I didn't share her enthusiasm.

"What about lasagna soup then?" she suggested.

"Not again!" Lexi cried. She crossed her arms over her chest and fell into a chair. "I am so tired of the same thing over and over."

Our mom swayed in her position, and she grabbed the refrigerator for support. Lexi's back was to her, but I saw the effort my mom put into remaining on her feet. I rushed over to her to catch her, but my mom stopped me. "I'm fine."

Lexi turned around, bewildered, with her arms still crossed. "What did I miss?"

"It's fine, honey," our mom reassured her. "My blood sugar must be a little low. I only need to eat something."

Lexi and I shared a look. Our mother hadn't almost passed out from "low blood sugar" until six months ago.

"Can we have cheese sandwiches?" I tried. I wasn't a huge fan of the gooey sandwiches, but I wanted my mom to rest soon.

"How about a cereal night?" Lexi chimed in.

Our mom's face fell. "I knew that was a bad idea the first time we did it. You need more nutrition."

Before my mom launched into a detailed outline about the way certain foods affected our bodies, I proposed, "Whole wheat blueberry pancakes?"

"Yay!" Lexi cheered.

Our mom frowned. "There's so much sugar in the syrup."

"You said that your blood sugar was low," Lexi referenced, moving her eyebrows up and down.

Our mom laughed at her display. "Okay, okay," she conceded. "We'll have breakfast for dinner."

"No chance for bacon with the pancakes?" I joked.

"I have Fakon," my mom teased.

I threw my hands up and huffed at the ceiling in mock disgust. My mom played back, patting me on the back and throwing in a "poor baby" to validate my simulated distress.

After dinner, I stayed in my room. Lexi watched a mind-numbing show about horses, and my mom practiced needlepoint.

I pulled my beef jerky from under my mattress and soundlessly peeled opened the bag. I chewed deliberately, letting the juices from the meat completely fill my mouth before I swallowed.

I replaced the bag, and my hand brushed the package. I had placed the vile of Scorn in a manilla envelope that had held a report of my grades. I'd stared at the vile for what seemed like hours but was probably only a handful of minutes. I'd asked myself the reason I was holding back and been thinking about the drug and its effects. Very gradually, I'd noticed movement. I'd blinked my eyes several times, but the likeness of the ouroboros on the vile continued to move, as if it was unlocking a secret. I'd shut my lids together forcefully, and when I'd opened them, the design was still. I had shoved it into the first thing I saw that would cover the drug without crushing it.

I shook off the memory of the image and reviewed my situation. My mom and sister were drinking herbal tea and chatting in the living room. *Could I get away with using it?*

My phone rang and startled me. I fumbled for the button to accept the call, eager to talk, but scared about what I should say.

"Hey."

"Hey," I responded awkwardly.

"I made the team," Loila informed me.

I thought of several answers. *I knew you could do it* and *I had no doubt* were quickly dismissed. Instead, I said, "Good."

Good! What was I thinking?

"Do you really think so?" she asked.

Something about her tone calmed my fear about my earlier response. "Yes," I stated more solidly. "It's good."

"Will you come to the games?"

I smiled. I didn't know how many games I could go to and escape the notice of the athletic jocks. They liked to point out anyone who was different, and my all-black attire didn't scream conformity.

"I'll go to *all* the games," I chuckled. If anyone messed with me, I'd fight them all.

———◇———

Trees flashed by me and whipped my face. The metallic taste of blood coated my mouth, and everything around me was muted in whites, blacks, and grays.

The brilliance of blood was almost blinding. I was drawn to it. I wanted to taste it again.

I woke up in a sweat that I was sure was a blood bath. I turned on the light quickly and discovered my soggy sheets. I grabbed my glasses off my dresser and stared in the mirror.

To my relief, there was no blood anywhere. I opened my mouth, and some of the beef jerky was stuck in my molars.

I wasn't disgusted about the possibility of blood in my mouth. In fact, it had felt natural. A stab of shame cut through my midsection. It was an unfamiliar feeling. Why should I be ashamed of a dream?

I wondered about the source of the blood. In my dream, I had thought it was the blood of an animal, but had it been human blood?

I shook the thought out of my head. "Mom's just going to have to let me eat meat again," I voiced to my empty room.

CHAPTER SEVEN

Loila ducked inside the cave, and I put down my jacket on a rock for her. She picked up my jacket and tossed it to me.

"A little dirt won't hurt me," she insisted.

I was grateful to have my jacket back. I had extended the chivalrous gesture without thinking about the cool temperature in the cave. It would still be another couple of months before it kept us cooler than the summer temperatures.

Loila grabbed her notebook and drew on it lazily. The cave had been our retreat since first grade, and no one bothered the stuff we left in it. It was nestled in a mountainside on the back end of Aiden's family's property, so there was very little chance of anyone finding it.

I watched her, waiting for an opportunity to make my friend laugh, or inch closer to her. She didn't seem to be aware of my gaze and was perfectly comfortable in my company. Loila scratched some of the purple nail polish off her chipped fingernails and appraised them. Her small mouth formed a pout, and then she returned to her drawing. I could have watched her all day. It was like seeing Aphrodite in her own home among her things.

Loila flicked some moisture off the cover of her notebook. "You don't think it will flood again, do you?"

I shook my head. There had only been one flood that had caused the river to rise enough to enter the cave. None of us had been able to get out of our houses, so we didn't know the cave had flooded until a week later.

A salamander slipped past her feet, and Loila appraised it. "I wish my mom would let me have pets," she commented.

Her family's dog had died, and it had been hard on Moira, Loila's younger sister. Her parents were unwilling to bring another pet into their home. Loila loved animals so much that we wondered if she would become a veterinarian.

"What kind of pet would you get?"

Loila looked up thoughtfully. "I loved my dog, but I think I would get a cat." She glanced down at the salamander. "I would have one of these guys, if they would let me hold them for more than ten seconds," she added. The salamander rewarded her attention by slithering away.

"How are the cheerleaders?" I asked.

"They're fine," she responded. She drew a dark star and traced over its outer edge.

I chanced an inquiry about the Rituals. "Have they asked you to do anything?"

Loila smiled. "No, I don't think they'll make me do more than cut my hair into bangs or pierce the cartilage on one of my ears."

I threw my friend under the bus. "Aiden was worried that they'd make you spend the night alone in Lost Cove, or something."

Loila stared at the mouth of the cave. Little droplets of rain were in harmony with rustling wind. She realized that I was still waiting for an answer. "I don't think they do things like that anymore," she spoke quickly. Loila stood and placed her notebook on a rock that jutted out like a small, uneven shelf.

Our quiet time in the cave was over. I had ruined it when I had asked about the Rituals. I was certain of one thing, though. Loila knew more about the Rituals than she was telling me, and it meant that I should be concerned. Very concerned.

CHAPTER EIGHT

Aiden pulled my shirt to stop me before I went into the gymnasium. "We need snacks, bro."

I waited while he ordered two nachos and two sodas. I opened my mouth to say that I'd pay him back, but he interrupted me.

"No, man. I got it all for me, but you can have some if you want it."

Aiden had found a clever way of buying me food without accepting recompense. It still wounded my pride when he placed the food and drinks between us. I wished that I had his money. I could buy all the food I wanted and get my mom the best medical care.

The cheerleaders filed out of the side entrance. Loila was the last one out, waving her pom poms wildly. She sat down with two other girls in a row of chairs behind the squad.

"I don't know why we have to be at a game if she's not even cheering," Aiden huffed.

"We're her friends," I reminded him. "We're here to support her."

I didn't like basketball. I enjoyed shooting baskets with my friends sometimes, but I didn't see the need to play the actual game. It was like engaging in Keep Away with the addition of hoops.

At half-time, Loila ran out onto the court with the other cheerleaders for their routine. She nailed every movement, but her smile was strained.

Aiden noticed it too. "Do you think she's nervous?"

"I don't know," I answered thoughtfully.

The second half of the game seemed to go by much faster than the first half. The energy in the room was almost tangible, but the spirit had no effect on Loila. She sat rigidly, eyeing the players automatically.

I didn't have the chance to talk to her after the game, and she didn't respond to my text. Aiden asked me to get a pizza with him, but I decided to go home.

My mom and sister were curled up on the couch. Monique sat in a chair beside the door.

"Did we win?" she asked.

I never understood the reference. It either joined us to a team to which we didn't belong or insinuated that we had strong feelings about the outcome of their score.

"I think Pale Woods Academy won," I replied.

My mom sat up. "If you're going to attend a game then you should know who won," she reproached. "Monique and I teach there, and you and Lexi attend that school. You have a vested interest in the outcome of the game."

"How does it affect me?" I chuckled. "Is it going on my permanent record if we lose to the Hornets?"

"No," Monique answered, "but you can have school spirit." She smiled before she finished her sentence. My mom had delusions of the type of teenager who lived with her, but Monique had a clearer idea about me.

They asked me to finish the movie with them, but I slinked down the hall with a half excuse. My window was open, and the room felt cold and moist. I slammed the window and locked it. *Had someone been in my room?*

I shoved my hand between my mattresses and pulled out the package. My hope for escape was still inside its plain manilla packaging. I had been so scared that I had lost it, or that I had been discovered, but whoever had opened the window had not uncovered my treasure.

I wondered who could have been in my room. I decided not to wait and let all my work to obtain it be for nothing. If I was going to use it, then I didn't need to keep it in my room where anyone could find it. I decided to use the powder in the vial the next day.

I tried to sleep, but nightmares threatened to cut my dreams with their raging claws. I finally gave up and embraced the night, flicking on the lamp on my nightstand. I pulled out the subject of my inner turmoil from between my mattresses.

I stared at the vial. It stared at me. I rolled the contents around the small container and watched the amber sands catch the light.

New drugs were developed every day—they hit the underground market almost immediately—but this one was different. Some said that it was the biggest high of their lives. others claimed that they could live on its euphoria forever.

No one questioned its origin. It had been made in a completely untraceable lab, so its source was not addressed. The government wanted to find a way to get it off the street, but the dealers moved in tight circles, never revealing themselves.

It was worth a fortune and was a drug for the elite that trickled down to the more socioeconomically disadvantaged. My mom couldn't pay for it with five years of her salary, yet small quantities leaked into the hands of people who had recent income tax refunds or decent savings accounts.

The how and why I got it were surreal memories, and the edges of them blurred against my everyday life. Had I been in the right place at the right time? Maybe. But I had been waiting for the opportunity, like a stray dog who studied potential places for its next meal.

The man with the limp had tossed a vial to me, but there may have been other people who didn't agree with his actions. Could another person have seen me grab the vial and tracked me down?

My fourteen-year-old mind convinced me that no one had seen my elaborate sleight of hand, and I had escaped unnoticed. Every day that passed with the product of my deception between my mattresses solidified my presumptions. I had my precious powder, and I was ready to use it, but would I have the chance?

CHAPTER NINE

Pale Woods Academy never got a new student in the middle of the school year. Our school wasn't like the public schools that had to accept kids as the adults in their lives relocated for business, financial, or safety reasons. This girl should have been placed on the list to begin classes next year, but she stood in front of the class, asking the teacher if she was in the right classroom.

She was fresh and pretty, with round eyes and dark hair that barely touched her delicate, pale shoulders, but there was something calculating about her. I knew that whoever had spotted me swiping the vial had sent her.

She called herself "Rowen", and she looked like any other eighth grader. She made friends easily, laughing with the athletic kids, and playing a flute with the band. It seemed like I was the only one who saw her eyes linger on each student before she dismissed them as a suspect. I didn't meet her gaze. I looked down at my shoes or feigned interest in one of Aiden's jokes.

Did Rowan know that she was here for me? I had been careful, but cameras were everywhere in the abandoned factory. Was she toying with me?

"She's such a nice girl," Loila remarked one day. "I'm going to invite her to my party."

Loila's parties were by the river where her grandparents lived. They allowed her to have twenty-five of the kids from school on their property for four hours. When it was warm, we walked along the sand or kayaked on the water. It was never warm enough to swim. On the years it rained, we played in the giant arcade room and bowling alley in their basement.

"Who's out this year?" Aiden asked, punching at the air in front of her playfully.

"Don't worry," she laughed. "It's not you."

I glanced up from my shoes. Loila misread my action, and added, "Or Razz."

Aiden talked to her about which cheerleaders would be at the party and begged her to invite only the girls who didn't have boyfriends. I kept pace with them, but I didn't add to the conversation.

"...and we all laughed, and she went home," Loila finished.

"What?" I asked automatically.

"Carrie passed her Ritual," Loila informed me. Rituals were trials, and it seemed like a new cheerleader's hazing was over. "They made her pierce her belly button." She rubbed her hand over her stomach. "It was crazy to watch."

"I bet there was so much blood!" Aiden commented. He cackled into the air maniacally. We laughed at his display.

"It was everywhere," Loila went on. "Carrie got through it, though. They used ice and a needle. I think one of the girls brought one of her mother's naval rings."

"Have they made you do anything yet?" I asked her.

Loila hesitated, but she kept a cheerful tone. "Not yet," she chirped, "but I'm waiting for them to tell me that I have to have purple streaks or go do cheers outside the courthouse."

"I'll post pictures," Aiden teased.

"Yeah, you won't," I said. "We have too much dirt on you."

"If it rained, my dirt would make twenty mudpies," he laughed.

"Hey, Razz," Loila interjected. "Did you finish Mr. Sam's assignment?"

"Not yet."

"It was simple," Loila said, aghast. "All you had to do was complete a Punnet Square."

I didn't tell her that I'd been sleeping with a small package beneath me. Or that I had dreams about blood that had trickled into my daytime thoughts.

"I'll finish it before she calls the role," I promised.

Monique delayed starting the class, almost like she knew that I needed the time to complete her assignment. She took the role absent-mindedly.

"What did you learn from the Punnet Square?" she asked.

"I learned that I'm adopted," Aiden called out. The class erupted in muted laughter.

I stole a glance at Tabitha, who pretended she was interested in looking out the window. She had completed the assignment, but her traits would only match her parents' purely by coincidence.

"That's cute, Aiden," Monique spoke without amusement, "but a Punnet Square should not be used to point to paternity or maternity. It only gives a percentage chance for certain traits based on the biological parents' traits."

"Mr. Sams!" Rowan called from the back of the room. Monique nodded to her. "I learned that there was a twenty-five percent chance that my parents would have a child with green eyes."

"I guess you were in that twenty-five percent," Monique smiled, nodding to Rowan's most notable feature.

"Punnet Squares help us visualize the connection of offspring to their parents. Certain physical characteristics are passed from the parent to the offspring."

"How about other characteristics?" I asked.

Monique was knocked off guard by my question. I had even stunned myself.

"You mean, like proclivity toward certain diseases?"

"Sure," I agreed, and decided to push farther. "And psychological illnesses."

Monique stared at me with a mixture of frustration and pity. "It's been proven that certain psychological diseases can be passed from parent to offspring," she responded carefully. "But Punnet Squares do not help with that measure."

"What about schizophrenia?" I pressed. I was pushing a boundary with my mom's friend.

Monique's posture relaxed when she found a loophole in my question. "That's a question for psychology class."

She lifted her gaze to include all the students in the classroom. "In our next lesson, we're going to discuss DNA sequences and how they affect the individual."

I had been bested. Monique wouldn't mention my line of questioning to my mom, but her refusal to answer my inquiry was a clear message to leave her out of my wondering thoughts. I let my questions settle into the back of my mind, where they usually sat, collecting like grains of sand on a beach.

CHAPTER TEN

"They *are* different," my mom insisted, holding my chin so that she could look at me better.

"Let me see," Monique sighed. She didn't grab my chin, but I complied.

My mom and I had almost been eye level, but Monique had to stare up at me. I noticed the rich coffee color of her eyes while she was studying mine.

"There's a trace of gold in them," she conceded.

"A trace," my mom hissed. "I could make a twenty-four karat necklace out of the gold in his eyes now!"

"Would you pawn it and buy me a steak?" I joked.

"Not funny," my mom returned.

"Eyes can change around puberty," Monique mentioned thoughtfully.

I had no intention of talking about my changing body with a couple of thirty-somethings.

"I gotta bounce," I announced.

"Bounce your butt to my car," Monique said. "I need to talk to your mother before we leave."

I grudgingly stalked to the door. Lexi was already waiting on me. She moved her face in my line of sight.

"They *are* different," she remarked.

I stared back at her blue-green eyes that had matched mine. "Maybe you'll get gold in your eyes one day."

"When I'm in the public?" she asked.

"What?"

"I heard Monique say that eyes can change around the public."

"That's not what she said," I chuckled, ruffling her hair.

She smoothed it back into place, only slightly annoyed. "Do you think mom will be okay?" she asked suddenly.

I thought about our mom's sudden weight loss and pale-gray skin. I had been worried about her, too.

"You know Mom," I told my sister. "She's too stubborn to die. She'll be okay."

"But what if she's not," Lexi pressed. "Who will take care of me?"

I knew what she wanted, and I gave it to her. "I'll take care of you, Lexi Lou." I added the nickname our father had called her.

My words were all the assurance she needed. She hugged me quickly and hopped to the door.

CHAPTER ELEVEN

Pale Woods Academy was buzzing with activity. During the announcements, the principal told the school there would be a guest speaker, and academics would be abbreviated. Usually, the smaller children would be the first to see a program, but the topic was of more importance to the upper classmen, so after the highschoolers left, I was among the second group of students who filed into the auditorium.

Signs hung on either side of the stage. Posters with the ouroboros the dealers stamped on every vile of Scorn were suspended by fishing line beside the signs with red X's slashed through them. The paint was a shade between crimson and ruby red, reminding me of blood. Candy apple letters shouted 'No way! Not Today!' against a white background. We had all chanted the mantra in fourth grade when an officer had led a program for our class each week that discussed the uses and abuses of drugs.

The principal, Georgia Bailey, stood at the podium and commanded silence with her posture. I had attended almost a decade of classes at Pale Woods Academy, and her fiery red hair and crystal blue eyes hadn't faded, even though she was well past sixty. She looked over the room to quiet any stray mumblings before she spoke.

"We are constrained by time," she began, "so your speaker will start her presentation immediately. Please welcome Lieutenant Mildred Bane."

Sporadic applause littered the room. A petit figure in a black pants suit strode confidently to the stage. Her name had not betrayed her age, and I was surprised to see a woman who appeared younger than my mom lift the mic on the podium and address us.

"We have a common enemy," she declared. Her opening statement was meant to stir us, but everyone was busy trying to find the best way to look at their phones without the teachers catching them.

"Scorn has infiltrated our community and diminished our ranks," she continued, as if we were soldiers under her command.

I was a little irritated by the speaker's approach. Sure, many of the students had lost a family member to Scorn, but she spoke about our town like she lived here, and I had never seen the woman at any of our shops or local hangouts.

"I used to go to this school, and my parents still sell produce by the river," she informed us. "I sat in the same auditorium, and I went to the Apple Festival in town every year. I left for the air force, and I didn't know I would find my hometown in such a mess when I came back."

A couple of kids looked around at each other. We didn't realize that the quality of our community had gone downhill.

"It starts out simple enough," Lieutenant Bane went on. "A couple of teenagers and young adults are given a small, diluted amount of Scorn to hook them." She walked across the stage, her boots making louder echoes than I had expected. "Once they're dependent on the drug, if they even live long enough"— she added under her breath— "they can be used to distribute Scorn to more young people." She pointed a finger into the audience. "They try to give the drugs to as many people as they can, because once those individuals are addicts, they become buyers. Buyers can give the dealers money to obtain Scorn for themselves.

"You see," she explained, "That's why it's so hard to end the cycle. Everyone who deals is an addict, and no one really knows the person responsible for distribution."

She had strayed off her main topic, but she picked it back up. "You are each young and healthy, but any drug can change that. Especially Scorn. Scorn alters your biological chemistry and creates a genetic need that will never be satisfied."

She stepped from one side of the stage to the other, gesticulating frequently and raising and lowering her voice to produce an effect that held the attention of the preteens in the room. "The drug attaches itself to your DNA, causing rapid biological changes and extending your telomeres. It works on your senses, making each one more acute. It extends your life by altering your DNA."

"Don't threaten me with a good time!" a male voice called from the back.

It was only a joke, but Lieutenant Bane narrowed her eyes into the crowd, searching for the offender. Her voice was barely a whisper at first, but it grew until it was larger than the auditorium. I didn't know who had called out, but by the time Lieutenant Bane finished, we all regretted the boy's outburst.

"Sure," she breathed in an amiable tone. "It all sounds like fun. You can smell pizza four blocks away. You can see individual leaves on a mountain's trees. You can taste every ingredient that went into a stew, and the dish soap that washed the pot before it was made."

She moved with the microphone, causing small interferences when she placed it too close to her mouth. There were lots of smiles and giggles until she spoke again.

"But then, your vision blurs and you start to hallucinate. You don't see people, your family, and your friends the same way. You smell food, but it hurts you to eat it. All you want is blood. So, all that desire to strengthen your senses and live a longer life crashes in on you. Once the task force catches you, you live off pig's blood in a kennel."

She was referencing the gated camps that held Scorn abusers. The government released what the prisoners were fed, but no one was allowed to visit them. The government wanted the public to believe that they were looking for ways to reverse the effects of Scorn, but no one had ever returned from the Scorn camps. No one.

She scoffed. "*Live*." She resumed pacing. "You exist. They can't let you back into society. You would be a terror."

We had all heard the horror stories. Friends ripped each other apart. Parents crushed their children's bones.

"They gave it to my uncle," a bold voice spoke. "He had been in a car wreck, and his spine was severed. The doctors gave it to him, and he walked out of the hospital in six days."

The kid's uncle must have been rich. Scorn was only administered medicinally if a person could pay a hefty sum.

Lieutenant Bane blinked and took a deep breath. "Under certain circumstances, small quantities can be administered in a medical setting."

"So, if you just take a little bit then your golden," Aiden called out.

I was embarrassed that he had spoken. I was sitting beside him, and I could feel eyes all over us.

"The kind that is used in the medical facilities is rigorously tested. The doctors match your blood type to be certain they can use it—"

"What blood type do you need to be?" someone shouted.

"You're missing the point!" Lieutenant Bane thundered, and I got the idea that if we had been in her unit, we would have all been doing pushups until our elbows buckled. She took a moment in the silence that followed to collect herself. "Even people who match the blood type can turn into monsters."

"I thought it was synthetic," a boy said in the front row. I recognized him from my science class. Monique always told me that I should be more like him since he made the best grades in the school. "You just said 'doctors match your blood type,' but if it was synthetic then a person's blood type wouldn't be a direct concern."

"There's some speculation that the drug was created organically."

She had stopped moving on the stage as she took our questions like she was standing before a firing squad. We had been her hardest group, but she wasn't giving up. I admired her perseverance.

"Imagine your friend told you that he went to a party and tried Scorn," she clarified, bringing us back to her main point. "You worried about him, but it was just one time, right? The next day, he's just sitting in class, but then he pops up and jumps out the window."

Lieutenant Bane was drawing upon past news stories. That incident had only happened thirty miles from the school.

"Or think about the poor little girl whose father practiced medicine. He sampled some Scorn when he went to a medical conference. He came home, and he thought everything was under his control. The police never found his daughter's body."

She had spoken about the event that had haunted our small town for a decade. Brian Williams had been a respected member of our small community, but he had not been able to withstand the effects of Scorn. His young daughter, Ophelia, had tried to prevent him from taking the drug. She had discovered his small stash, and she had hidden it.

Dr. Williams told the authorities that he had been enraged when he discovered his drugs were missing. He had confronted Ophelia, and she admitted that she had hidden them. He remembered his rage, but he couldn't tell the police what had happened to his daughter.

They handcuffed him, but Dr. Williams broke free of the bonds. He left in search of his missing daughter, or to hide from the police, or both.

"...and the tests proved that the blood was Ophelia Williams'," Lieutenant Bane was saying.

My mom had told me about it. After the police had found Ophelia's blood on a part of the Appalachian Trail near our small town, my mom had kept me inside. My father must have been worried too, because he stayed home more often in the time that followed Dr. Williams's escape.

Lieutenant Bane had restored her control over the students in the room, so she went through a couple of exercises that she thought would strengthen our understanding about the impact of drug use. Aiden was called to participate, so I settled in for a show. He didn't disappoint me, and the entire auditorium exploded over the mockery he made of Mildred Bane when her back was turned. She sensed his trickery, but she didn't catch him. She decided to face him, and the joking stopped.

She called for volunteers for the next exercise. Aiden had just returned to his seat, and he flung my hand up.

"You get a piece of candy if you volunteer," he declared, holding his small chocolate up as proof.

I jerked my hand back down, but not before Lieutenant Bane zeroed in on it. She surveyed me and beckoned me to the stage.

"It better be the best candy in the world," I hissed at Aiden when I moved past him. He responded by showing me his chocolate-covered teeth.

There were only two volunteers on the stage, and neither of us looked willing. Tabitha crossed her arms over her midsection, and I followed her gaze. Several cheerleaders sniggered around an empty seat. Loila sat beside the unoccupied chair, staring miserably at the stage. Tabitha wasn't a cheerleader, but as Loila's best friend, she had been bullied into volunteering.

"When I talk, do actions that illustrate my words," she instructed Tabitha and me. "I may say drop your hands"—she turned to Tabitha, and she complied—"or jump up and down"—she pointed at me.

I didn't want to move, but Lieutenant Bane's stare was fierce. I finally decided that I would do what she asked to get Tabitha and me off the stage as fast as possible. There was some muffled laughter when I bounced up and down, but most of the students hadn't been paying attention.

"At first, the effects of Scorn are subtle to our loved ones," Lieutenant Bane explained, commanding the attention of the audience again. "There may be some increased aggression, or dietary differences."

She turned to me. I threw my hand up in a claw, and then pretended to shovel food into my mouth from an imaginary plate.

Laughter erupted. Lieutenant Bane had expected it, and she smiled benignly. She placed her arm around Tabitha, put the microphone close to her lips, and whispered, "But then the changes truly begin."

I wasn't certain if an action was required of me, so I stood still. Mildred Bane threw her hand into the air, and a tear slid down Tabitha's cheek. She wiped it away quickly.

"Maybe you've seen them backed against the wall, like a wild, cornered animal," she went on, her voice rising.

I held back a moment before I crouched low and held my hands up. Lieutenant Bane shook her head at me. I understood her meaning, and I dropped into my assigned character. My only intention was to get Tabitha off the stage before she cried in front of the school. I drew my face into a snarl, and I held an attack position.

She was satisfied with my representation. "The love you knew is gone, and only a dark, hostile thing remains."

Lieutenant Bane grabbed Tabitha's shoulder again. This time, she meant to hold her in place. "Then your friend, brother, or *father* attacks, and you don't remember anything but the blood."

No one had ever mentioned to me that Tabitha had survived an attack. I hadn't heard that her aunt and uncle had adopted her after she had witnessed her father kill her mother and she had narrowly escaped with her life. I didn't know about her fear, or the even deeper secret beneath all the others, but Lieutenant Bane did.

I played my part well. I locked my eyes on Tabitha and moved my snarl up my face until I was consumed in mock fury. I lunged at her.

I never came close to her, but Tabitha wailed. She ducked out of Lieutenant Bane's hold and ran off the stage. She threw her hands up to prevent the audience from witnessing her tears, but it caused her to trip on the stairs. She tumbled down, like a child's discarded doll, and landed on her side. She grabbed her shoulder and limped away before well-meaning students could help her.

Loila sprang from her seat. She cast a disapproving look on the cheerleaders who were overtaken by laughter before she ran after Tabitha.

Lieutenant Bane handed me two pieces of chocolate for my performance. "Give the other one to your little friend," she told me. A smirk danced across her lips.

I threw the chocolate at Aiden's chest when I got back to my seat. He looked at me incredulously, but he didn't retaliate. I couldn't talk to him. Anything I said would result in a string of language they didn't allow at Pale Woods Academy.

I was a social pariah the rest of the day. I tried to talk to Loila, but she wouldn't even acknowledge me. I finally approached Tabitha, but she screamed and ran away. Loila held her and shouted at me to go away.

I learned later that Tabitha had experienced night terrors about people on Scorn, and in a couple of moments, I had unwound years of intensive therapy. I couldn't believe that my attempt to help Tabitha get off the stage had marked me as a monster.

I heard them halfway down the hall, and I my face flamed red with shame. Loila soothed Tabitha while she whimpered, "Did you see him? He looked just like one of them."

CHAPTER TWELVE

I sent Loila countless texts over the next few days, but she never responded. I returned a pencil she had dropped in class to her, and she stared icicles at me.

I decided to let her forgive me on her own. I hung out at our cave in the afternoons, hoping that she would drop in after cheerleading practice, but she never showed up. Instead, Aiden and I spent the evenings talking while his father was away.

"Where is your father this week?" I asked.

Aiden stared into his bag of ranch flavored chips. "I think he's in Chicago, but he could be in China, for all I know."

I was stunned by his statement, but I didn't say anything. I had been the one to bring up an uncomfortable subject.

I was prepared to talk about something else, but Aiden jumped up and walked to the mouth of the cave. He clutched the chip bag tightly as he stared in the direction of his house.

I tried to do anything that didn't make me seem like I was conscious of his internal struggle. I flicked a rock, but I decided that it made too much noise, so I put my hands together.

Finally, I resigned myself to watching Aiden's frustration rise up to the surface and explode. When it did, I could hardly look at him as tears glossed his eyes and spittle with bits of chip flew from his mouth.

"Would it kill him to stay home longer than a couple of days at a time?" he began.

I stared at my shoes. I searched my mind for a conversation to derail his train of thought, but he kept running down the track.

"I mean, it's not like he has to put diapers on me, or something," he expressed. "I don't expect him to play catch in the yard." Aiden motioned to the direction of his property. "I just want to go to the movies with him once in a while or eat dinner with him a couple of nights a week."

I met Aiden's eyes, but I remained silent. I had nothing to offer. "That sucks, man" was not going to make him feel better.

Aiden looked back out of the cave miserably, as if the darkening sky could provide solace. "It was hard with her around, but at least she paid attention to me," he whispered.

My ears perked up at the mention of his mother. She had died before Aiden and I were close friends.

He threw the chip bag into the depths of the cave. At that moment, I would have done or said anything to keep him from crying. I just didn't know what words or actions would keep it from happening.

Luckily, Aiden didn't want to cry, but he was angry. He kicked rocks, and slung small boulders into the cave. His anger was fierce as he propelled heavy boulders farther down the cave than we'd explored. I worried he might hurt himself, but when he didn't succeed in loosening a larger rock from just outside the cave, I became less anxious. He slumped against the rock, red-faced and panting.

He looked at me and shouted, "Well, don't you have anything to say?"

I stared back at him and said the only thing that came to my mind. "At least your dad comes back."

It was like I had splashed cool water on him. His posture relaxed, and he dropped his eyes.

"Oh, dude, I forgot."

I tried to turn his focus away from me. "It's no big deal," I said, waving away his pity. "It was a long time ago."

"My mom OD'd when I was little, but it's still a big deal," he compared. "I shouldn't have said all that stuff about my father in front of you. It would be like you saying something bad about your mom in front of me."

"It's all good."

Aiden scooted up onto the large rock, and the conversation finally veered toward a safer topic. "When do you think Loila will start talking to you again?"

I shrugged. "Probably when Tabitha forgives me."

"I don't get it." Aiden sniffed. "You only did what the speaker told you to do. It's not your fault that Tabitha had some sort of issue with it. She shouldn't have volunteered to go on stage if she knew it was going to bother her."

"The cheerleaders made her do it."

Aiden cut his eyes at me. "She's not part of the squad," he pointed out. "How can they make *her* do anything?"

"She's Loila's friend," I explained. "Tabitha's probably worried that she'll get Loila kicked out if she doesn't do what they say."

"Or they'll make Loila stop hanging out with her," Aiden added, understanding my point.

⸺◆⸺

I was glad that Aiden hadn't tried to express any more of his feelings, but his outburst bothered me. I thought about it on my way home and through dinner.

I volunteered to wash the dishes so my mom could grade papers. After I finished, I plopped down on the couch.

"Shh!" my mom hissed. Lexi was asleep on the other end of the couch with her mouth open.

I nodded and lifted my sister. My mom started to protest, but then she allowed me to carry Lexi to her bed.

I rejoined my mom in the living room. I opened an app on my phone so I could change the channels on the television. My mom sat down beside me and curled into me. I hadn't really liked for her to hold me that way since I became a teenager, but I felt sorry for her. She had been given a death sentence, and Monique, Lexi, and I were her only comfort.

Halfway into a movie about schizophrenia and aliens, I asked her, "What happened to Aiden's mom?"

"She overdosed," my mom replied simply.

I pulled away from her embrace, and settled into a straighter posture, giving her my full attention.

"Savannah and I were friends in school," she added. "She always had a substance abuse problem."

"Was it Scorn?" I asked carefully.

My mom took a deep breath. "It wasn't Scorn back then. She took nerve pills."

"Oh," I said. I thought the conversation was over until my mom measured me with her eyes and began again.

"She was a little anxious after Aiden was born, so her doctor prescribed her some nerve pills to help her stay calm. At first, Savannah seemed fine.

She was devoted to Aiden, and she took him to the park and had nice birthday parties for him. We had a few playdates with them."

My mom looked back into a memory. I watched her face for signs that she was sugar-coating the truth, but she spoke to me evenly and honestly.

"Savannah was okay until she wasn't," my mom remembered. "She went on first grade field trips and signed Aiden up for soccer one day, and the next day she was nodding out at a parent-teacher conference."

Realization dawned on me. "Aiden was in your class when she died."

My mom nodded solemnly. "She dropped him off at the door to my class that morning. She hugged him and told him that he was her world. By lunch, Aiden's father had picked him up. It hadn't taken them long to find her and move her body out of the house."

"Do you think that she knew what she was going to do?" I asked. "She told him he was her whole world before she left him."

My mom shook her head. "Savannah told him that every morning. And I don't think she had planned to die. She didn't want Aiden's father to have him."

"He doesn't pay attention to him," I confided.

"It's a little more than that," my mom said.

She turned her attention back to the movie, and she didn't try to cuddle me. I had the feeling that I hadn't asked an important question, but I couldn't think of anything else to say.

I tried to enjoy my time with my mom without thinking about Aiden's relationship with his parents, my mom's illness, or the vial of Scorn between my mattresses. I tried to be unconcerned about the possibility that someone had been sent to spy on me at my school or that Loila was mad at me. I tried not to think about anything past the end of the movie, because the end of something is always the start of something else, and it's not always good.

CHAPTER THIRTEEN

There wasn't any blood. It seemed to me that there should be blood since the injury had happened inside her body. I could see her bone poking inside her skin at an odd angle, but nothing else about her condition was abnormal.

A well-meaning pedestrian called 911. I sat next to my sister helplessly while she screamed. I tried to concentrate on her and take some of her pain away, but it didn't work. She cried. She held onto her leg pitifully, but she couldn't grab her arm. It hurt too much.

The ambulance took forever to arrive. The EMS worker took eons gathering information about Lexi and the accident before they finally put her on a stretcher.

"Were you present at the time of the incident?" they asked me.

"It was all my fault," I responded, but it wasn't enough for them. They had me rehash every terrible moment.

The nurses wouldn't let me stay with my sister when we got to the hospital. They said Lexi needed x-rays, so I wouldn't be able to be with her anyway.

Her screams echoed down the hall. "Razz! Razz! I want my brother!"

I didn't deserve her cries. I was the reason for her pain.

I found a chair in the family waiting room and I put my head in my hands. The hospital called my mom, and she found me.

"What happened?"

"I think her arm is broken," I choked out.

I didn't want to cry. I didn't deserve to cry, but the tears threatened anyway.

My mom put her arm around me. "Everything will be okay, Razzberry," she spoke. "The nurse told me that her arm is broken, but we'll be able to see her soon."

"It's my fault," I shouted. A couple of people glanced in our direction before they realized that I wasn't going to make a scene. "It was my fault," I said more quietly.

My mom's mouth formed a thin line, not judging me or relieving me of my guilt. "Tell me how she broke her arm."

I looked at my hands. "She was playing in the park," I recounted. "She was on the jungle gym, and she wanted me to watch her. I told her to wait a minute, because I was on the phone with Aiden, so she stayed at the top. She must have waited ten more minutes before she tried to get down."

"You weren't watching her for ten minutes?"

"No, I could see her," I defended. "I knew that she was at the top of the jungle gym, so I thought she would be okay until I finished talking to Aiden."

My mom nodded. "Did she fall?"

"Yeah," I answered. "She yelled at me to show me how she could balance along the top of the jungle gym. I had walked father away to have privacy when I talked to Aiden. I wasn't close enough to the jungle gym to catch her."

"Razzberry—" my mom started.

"No, mom," I spoke. "It's *my* fault."

"Well, let's say it's your fault. You can take the blame for walking too far away from her, but can you say that you would have caught her if you had been just outside the jungle gym?"

"I would have had a better chance of it," I countered.

"Maybe," my mom replied. "If you had been there, but you hadn't moved fast enough to catch her, would you still be so hard on yourself?"

My mom was trying to rationalize with me, but I was in no mood to humor her way of thinking. "It was my fault," I repeated defiantly.

An hour later, my sister's name was announced at the doorway to the waiting room. My mom popped up, and I followed her. The nurse verified our relationship to his patient before he relayed her condition.

"Lexi is going to be fine," he told us. "She had a non-displaced radial fracture. She will wear a cast for four to six weeks, and she should be able to do everything she could do before in about three or four months."

"No surgery?" my mom inquired.

"No," the nurse confirmed. "Most people call it a broken arm, but it is only a fracture. It should heal nicely."

I was in shock. I thought my sister's bone had been oddly pressed against her skin. Had my mind exaggerated the injury?

"Where is she?" my mom said. "Can we see her?"

The nurse led us though hallways which were second nature to him and a maze to us. My sister had just been placed in the room, and another nurse was adjusting the wires they attached to her. The nurses exchanged a look that told me that they knew each other more than professionally.

Lexi had been given a sedative, and she rested, sitting up, with her mouth hanging open. She had a bright pink cast on her arm, and I wondered how mad she would be about it when she woke. She hated pink.

My mother rushed to the side of the bed, and the nurse smiled at her. She tossed a glance at me. "Are you Razz?"

"Yeah," I responded, keeping my position just inside the door.

"She's been asking about you," the nurse informed me.

The nurse who had led us to my sister's room received a call on a device on his shirt. He waved to me and ducked out of the room.

My mom was praying over my sister in hushed whispers. She had started crying the moment she saw Lexi on the hospital bed.

"I'm finished over here," the nurse announced. "You can come over and sit on this side of your sister." Her words were meant to direct me to my sister's bedside.

The nurse misunderstood my hesitation. "It's okay," she soothed. "You won't bother any of the machines."

I walked automatically to the place the nurse indicated. She put one hand on each of my arms. It was a little awkward for me, but I allowed the touch.

I had the feeling that the nurse was waiting for me to talk to Lexi. I wasn't going to speak to my sister in front of an audience, but I placed my hand on her shoulder. I was surprised when she stirred.

"See," the nurse confirmed. "She was waiting on you."

My mom looked up when my sister moved. "Do you really think she responded to him?"

"Yes," the nurse replied, rubbing one of my arms. "I used to work with coma patients, and you'd be surprised by the way they'd respond to different family members. For instance, there was this little girl who stayed in a coma for a month after a trip down the stairs. The mother read to her and held her hand, but the father would visit for an hour once a day, and the little girl would move her fingers at least once while he was there. It turned out that the mother had pushed the little girl down the stairs."

"I wasn't there when she fell off the jungle gym," my mom quickly defended, anxious about a comparison of the injuries.

"It was my fault," I added.

The nurse sensed my melancholy and turned me to face her. "Did you push her?"

"No, but I was on my phone, and—"

The nurse stopped me. "It was an accident," she insisted. "People are using their phones much more than they should, but it doesn't mean that you were responsible for the accident. Your sister could have fallen off the jungle gym, even if you were giving her your full attention."

Her words comforted me very little, even though I knew they were true. She rubbed my arm again and asked my mom if she could get us anything. My mom said we were okay, but the nurse quickly returned with two clear sodas.

"I'm Caroline," she told us. "I will be Lexi's nurse until the shift changes tonight."

Lexi dozed in and out for the rest of the afternoon and into the night. A food tray arrived for my sister, but my mom told me to eat it. Lexi couldn't keep her eyes open.

Lexi woke up early the next morning. My mom and I were on either side of her, slumped in the chairs where we had slept.

I squeezed her hand, "Hey, kid."

"You stayed," she smiled.

"Yeah," I returned. "I had to make sure that you didn't take a dive off the building."

Lexi tried to laugh, but her throat was hoarse. I rushed to get her a choice of water or fruit juice. She chose hesitantly, watching my moves. Perplexed, she asked, "What's wrong?"

"Nothing," I replied automatically. I gave her the orange juice she had picked, but I took it back quickly to open it for her.

"You're acting weird."

"You're in a hospital bed," I said, as if it explained everything.

Lexi shook her head. "It wasn't your fault, you know."

I kept my face expressionless and nodded. I didn't commit to a feeling.

"I was the one who decided to walk across the top of the jungle gym."

I decided to infuse the situation with humor. My sister and I were the only ones awake in the room, but it made me uncomfortable to talk to her about my mistake.

"Yeah, Pinky, you never should have debuted a new balancing act without my full attention," I chuckled.

Lexi crinkled her eyebrows. "What do you mean *Pinky?*"

I nodded to her cast. Lexi's eyes widened.

"Why is it *pink*?" she demanded. "Did *you* tell them to put a pink cat on me?"

"The doctors chose it," our mom interjected, waking and stretching. "They probably put pink casts on every girl with broken bones."

Lexi scoffed. "Tell them to change it."

My mom had slept sitting up in a chair all night and she hadn't eaten. She was in no mood to humor my sister. "It won't be on your arm long enough for it to matter," she grumbled.

Lexi groaned when our mom told her that the cast would be on for at least a month and a half. I helped a little when I asked to be the first to sign it. My sister was much happier with her cast after I put my specialized signature on the top of it.

The doctor released her that afternoon, and Monique met us at our apartment. She looked more concerned than I expected. She hugged me and I could smell Philly cheesesteak from her lunch on her clothes.

Lexi limped into the house, even though there was nothing more than a couple of bruises on her legs. Monique appraised her.

"I may need to help her in the shower," my mom told her friend.

"That's okay," Monique replied. "I need to go back to the school. I just wanted to be sure Lexi was okay."

"I can help you grade papers if you need it," my mom offered. "I'll be sitting at home with Lexi today."

"I can do it!" Monique snapped.

My mom was stricken. I had never heard Monique raise her voice in class or in our home.

"I guess I was more on edge about Lexi than I thought," she apologized. She addressed my sister. "I'm glad you're okay."

My mom put her arm around my sister and squeezed her shoulder. Lexi gave Monique a half hug and winced from the effort. My mom and I glanced at each other, silently agreeing that my sister was milking her injury.

Monique and I hadn't hugged since I was ten. She respected my space, and offered a fist bump or a shoulder pat. Before she left, her mouth moved into a hard line, and she embraced me. I threw up my arms in surprise.

"I'll be by later," Monique promised. She moussed Lexi's hair. "Try to take it easy on your mom."

"No promises," Lexi teased.

My mom put Lexi in the shower and stayed to help her. I was instructed to make my sister's favorite lunch. It had to be timed perfectly, so I didn't press the bread into the toaster until my sister hobbled to the couch. I still couldn't understand how a broken arm had affected her legs.

I spread peanut butter over the warm bread, and it melted. I added a cup of applesauce and milk to her tray and put it over my sister's lap.

"You didn't cut it into a heart," Lexi whined.

The heart-shaped cookie cutter was in the drawer, but I had purposely ignored it. My sister could cut a heart into her sandwich if she wanted it.

I was happy to fall onto my bed, and I didn't even pull the sheets around me. I was almost asleep when I smelled it. A whiff of Philly cheesesteak.

I shot up out of bed and my hand dove between my mattresses, pulling out empty fingers. I turned my top mattress over and looked at the bare space where I had left the manilla envelope with the vial in it. There was no need to search the rest of my room. My Scorn was gone.

CHAPTER FOURTEEN

I thought about going straight to the school and confronting Monique. What would I have said, though?

Did you take my Scorn? Where did you put it?

I couldn't help wondering why Monique had gone through my stuff. She had never been more than a bystander in my upbringing. She would silently survey her ragged nails or busy herself with a needless task when my mom disciplined me, and when my mom stared at her for back up, she was phlegmatic.

She would probably tell my mom. In fact, she would have already ratted me out if Lexi hadn't just gotten home from the hospital.

I waited for my mom to call me to the kitchen. I was nervous about the consequences, but I was more concerned about my mom's disappointment.

The day dipped into evening, and Monique didn't join us for dinner. I chanced asking my mom about her.

"Monique sent me a text," my mom informed me. "She has a headache, so she won't be back tonight."

I didn't want anyone to suffer, but I was grateful for Monique's headache. It gave me more time to plan what I was going to tell my mom when she asked me about the Scorn I had hidden in my room. I readied multiple responses, and I acted out scenarios in my mind. I decided to lie about the way I got it and hope that my punishment didn't match my actions.

The weekend flew by, and Monique didn't visit us. She called to check on Lexi, but she didn't share meals with us or drop by for a couple of hours to give my mom some time to herself. I was surprised when I walked in on my family watching television Sunday night with Monique sitting in her usual chair.

On Monday, instead of riding with Monique and Lexi, I took a bus to school. It made an early pass at our apartment, so I avoided an uncomfortable exchange with my mom in front of Monique about my reasons.

At school, I avoided Monique as much as possible. When I was in her class, I absorbed the lessons, but I wouldn't allow her to force me into being vocal about my scientific observations. Monique noticed the difference.

I finally realized that Monique wasn't going to tell my mom. She probably thought that she could give me a tough love talk when the time was right, and I would drop my idea about using the drug.

Since she wasn't going to alert my mom about my transgression, I started riding to school with Lexi and her again. I didn't like getting up earlier to catch the bus.

The temperature was a little warmer for early spring, so our steps were lighter as we walked from the teacher's parking lot to the school. Monique twirled the keys around her fingers. She wasn't like other women who liked designer handbags. She kept her personal items in her pocket, in her hands, or locked in her desk at school.

"Have you talked to Faith?" she asked my sister.

"Yeah, I made up with her," Lexi commented, skipping beside us. She showed us her friend's name on her cast. "She drew an ugly bird next to her name."

I surveyed the small robin next to the girl's curly script. My sister had always hated birds. My mom said it was because she was like a cat, but Lexi told us that their beady eyes irritated her.

In front of us, the carpool line picked up speed now that the bell to signal the start of the school day was minutes away. We weren't worried about making it to our classes on time. Monique would write us an excuse if we were late.

Lexi was still scrutinizing the names on her cast, and she almost walked in front of a car. Monique moved so fast to push my sister out of harm's way that she was almost a blur.

I stood beside the scene, unmoving. I realized quickly that Lexi was okay, but there was more than the accident that plagued my thoughts. I replayed the incident in my head twelve times that day. No human I knew could move that fast.

It was then that I realized Monique hadn't taken my Scorn to keep it from me. She took it so she could use it.

CHAPTER FIFTEEN

After I concluded that Monique had stolen my Scorn for herself, I started to notice other little things. She was slightly more aggressive, she moved faster, and she had avoided the assembly about Scorn. *How long had she been using it?*

Some people could use Scorn for months without the knowledge of their family and friends. When they became dependent on the drug, the effects were usually fast and consuming, with tragic outcomes.

I watched Monique closely every day. I catalogued every movement and every word. One day after class, I worked up my courage to confront her, but someone stopped me.

"How's your sister?" she asked.

It was the first time Loila had spoken to me since the Scorn assembly. I was flustered, but I managed an easy response.

"She's itching under her cast, so she's begging our mom to have the doctors take it off."

"But it's only been two weeks," Loila commented.

My heart fluttered when I realized that Loila had kept up with my family, even though she was mad at me. I struggled to find another way to keep the conversation going.

"Have the cheerleaders given you a rite of passage yet?"

I had hoped to get a laugh and a story about a small inconvenience, like the pain from a piercing or a prank that Loila had to play on one of the teachers. Instead, Loila's posture stiffened, and she shook her head.

I tried to think of any other conversation that would keep Loila in front of me, but I had bruised my chance. She made an excuse and left before I could say anything more.

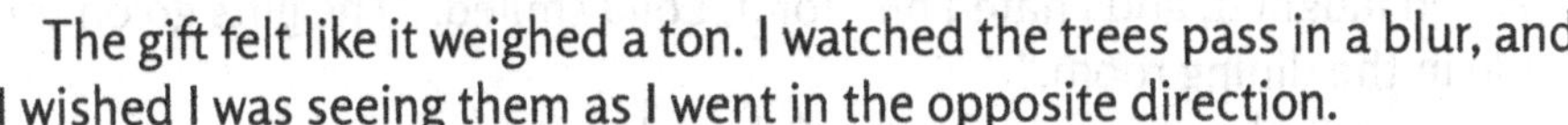

The gift felt like it weighed a ton. I watched the trees pass in a blur, and I wished I was seeing them as I went in the opposite direction.

After our last conversation, I doubted that I would be on the list for Loila's birthday party, but the invitation had arrived five days ago. In the past, her grandmother had always sent me the same manilla invitations embossed with their family crest over two weeks in advance, so I wondered if Loila had added my name at the last minute. It was hard for me to guess the status of our friendship, so I asked Aiden to ride along with me.

"Can we listen to the Lil' Pain song you like?" he asked my mom from his seat next to Lexi.

"It's Lil' *Wayne*," my mom chuckled.

"No! Rich Kids!" Lexi called from the back. She claimed it was our favorite song, and she made our mom play it every time we were in the car together.

My mom played both songs in the time it took us to reach the homes that were built alongside the river. The black iron gate was open, and I recognized Loila's parent's SUV.

"Why do they have a gate in their driveway?" Aiden asked. "Anyone can drive around it on either side if they want to get in."

"I think they just want to deter unannounced visits," my mom said.

"Oh, well, my dad has a big iron fence around our grounds."

Iron is expensive, and everyone isn't as rich as your dad, I thought.

Loila was at the door, greeting each guest. My heart landed in my stomach.

"Have fun!" my mom called, and she drove around the circular driveway. I could hear Lexi whining as they pulled away.

"C'mon dude," Aiden encouraged me. "Loila invited you. She's not gonna bite your head off."

I didn't think Loila was going to be outwardly mean to me, but I worried about her true feelings. Did she really consider me a friend, or had her grandparents automatically added me to the list since I had been at her parties in the past?

I pretended to listen to Aiden on the way up the concrete steps. It didn't seem forced since Aiden was always going on about something.

Loila held out her hand to the girl in front of me. "I'm glad you could make it," she spoke.

Had her eyes darted to me?

The girl moved on, and I had to take my place in front of Loila. She extended her hand. "I'm glad you could make it."

I was so nervous that I placed my gift in her hand. "You too," I muttered.

Aiden laughed, and I hated him for it. Loila smiled. "The gifts go on the table in the dining room."

I swiped the present out of her hand, muttered something unintelligible, and stalked down the hall. I found the table, tossed the gift onto it, and walked out the back door.

Half a dozen kids were in the pool, hitting each other with pool noodles and passing a beach ball. I hadn't even entertained the idea of getting in the water, leaving my swim trunks at home in the back of my drawer. Aiden had worn his swim trunks under his clothes, and he flew past me to cannon ball into the pool.

"Watch it!" a girl scolded from beside me. She had dropped her towel, so I bent over to pick it up. I was ready to apologize for my friend's impulsiveness when I realized that the girl was Rowan.

"Razz," she said coolly. She motioned for me to walk with her, and I obliged. We stepped down a set of stairs that emptied onto the sandy beach that lined the river. A couple of kids had taken a rowboat out to the middle of the lake. I watched one of them dive into the water after a lost oar and emerge shivering.

Rowan took off her loose-fitting shirt, exposing slender shoulders and a toned belly. She expected me to appraise her, but she'd made me uncomfortable. It almost felt like she was looking at me out of a more mature set of eyes.

"What are you doing here?" I asked before I could think.

Rowan waved my question in the air. "My sister knows Loila's grandparents. They want us to be the best of friends." She spoke about their hopes in a wind-swept voice, batting her eyelashes and widening her eyes, and then indicated her revulsion to the idea by pretending to gag herself.

"Loila's great," I defended.

"Oh, I'm sure. I'm just not much for being set up with people. I make my *own* choices," she asserted, looking at me pointedly.

"Okay, well, I'm going back to the pool with Aiden," I said, making a speedy retreat.

I didn't mind when girls flirted with me, but there was something underneath her words. Rowan was trying too hard to get my attention.

I climbed the steps without looking up, and I almost ran into Loila. She made a big show of going down the steps, even though it looked like she had been on her way to the beverage table with soft drinks. I guess it was easier for her to lug the two liters up and down the stairs than it was for her to admit that she had been watching my exchange with Rowan.

"Do you need help?"

Loila looked down at the sodas in her hands, "No, I'm just carrying these"— she left off, searching for a reason to be carrying the drinks down the stairs— "for the people on the beach," she finished.

"Do you need me to get cups?" I pushed, causing Loila to fully commit to her excuse.

"No," she responded, coloring. "I'll get those in a minute."

I turned around to look for Aiden, giving Loila time to sneak back up the stairs and dart to the beverage table.

It amazed me how easy it was to be alone when you were surrounded by people. I lounged in a beach recliner in the shade of an umbrella and navigated the social media on my phone, liking the pictures from people at the party, but never actually talking to them. Loila had a cake, but her friends weren't expected to stand around her while she blew the candles out. Her grandmother busied herself by handing out triangle-shaped portions of moist chocolate cake with blue and white icing. Her grandmother saw me alone in the outdoor recliner and patted my leg sympathetically. She had given me a piece with a light blue L, presumably the piece that had been part of Loila's name. I decided to let it mock me for a moment before I ate it.

Loila's grandparents had a heated pool, and the temperature was in the mid-seventies, so almost everyone was sweating. Only the kids that had stayed next to the river seemed cool from the breezes off the mountains.

Aiden shook himself off on me and moved away when I kicked at him. "It's time for her to open presents," he announced.

I obediently followed him into Loila's grandparent's living room. It was a sizable place, with a cathedral ceiling and a floor to ceiling window that showcased the perfect view of the Nolichucky River.

Presents of every size littered the table and floor. All twenty-five guests had gotten Loila a gift, and her parents promised a big surprise for her after she had opened all the other presents.

One by one, Loila tore open the packages. She smiled and thanked each of her guests. She was so genuine that I couldn't tell if she liked her coloring with diamonds book or the designer purse Aiden had brought for her better. Her parents had shown her the way to be gracious, and they nodded with the appreciation she showed each of her guests.

The number of presents dwindled, but I didn't see her open my gift. I scanned the remaining presents, but I couldn't find mine. I started to panic. *Had it fallen under the table? Had it been kicked under a chair?*

Finally, the last present was opened. *Where was my gift?!*

Loila's parents assumed that she was finished unwrapping the birthday presents from her friends, and they dangled keys in front of her eyes. Her grandparents told her that a new jet ski was waiting for her at the dock.

Loila was so excited that she ran out of the room, hastily throwing farewells and appreciation. Her parents dismissed themselves with their daughter so they could see her try out her new jet ski. It was understood that the party was over, and the guests started to leave.

"What did you get her, bro?" Aiden asked me.

"My present wasn't there. I don't know what happened to it."

We couldn't look around, because people would think we were trying to steal something, so we filed out the door. My mom was waiting for us.

"How was the party?"

I couldn't match her cheery disposition, so I let Aiden answer her. "It was pretty fun, Mrs. K. There was a nacho tower."

Of course Aiden would gage the success of a party on its food. His adolescent metabolism wouldn't allow him to stop eating.

"Did Loila like the ring?"

I had shown my mom the ring I had purchased for Loila. Mr. Shelton, the man who owned the pawn shop, had his niece pick out the ring for me. She seemed to have an eye for jewelry, and Loila loved emeralds, so I didn't worry about the price. It had cost me all the money I had saved from the lawns I had mowed in the summer. My mom had gushed over the ring, and she had helped me wrap the box in the pretty gold paper that we had saved from Christmas.

"You got her a ring, dude?" Aiden stopped fastening his seatbelt to stare at me with his mouth open.

"It's just a regular ring."

"An emerald ring is hardly *regular*," my mom interjected.

I raised my eyebrows at Lexi, begging her for a distraction, but she was mad at me for going to a party without her. She stuck her tongue out at me.

"It doesn't matter anyway," Aiden said. "It was lost before Loila opened it."

"You need to go back in and find it!" my mom commanded me, preparing to stop the car.

Sweat beaded across my forehead. I couldn't imagine going back inside to look around Loila's grandparent's place. "It's fine, Mom. Everyone's at the river with Loila's jet ski. They're going to look for it later."

My mom accepted my explanation, even though part of it was untrue. Loila and her family were unaware of the missing ring. She understood that I didn't want to go through a person's home while they were otherwise occupied. Instead, she asked, "Why are they letting her ride the jet ski on the river?"

"They aren't letting her ride it," Aiden piped up, chomping a bag of Cheetos he had swiped from the party. "Her grandparents have a place on Watauga Lake. Their summer house is two or three houses down from the place my dad just bought there."

My mom cringed. She didn't allow Lexi and me to eat food in the car, but she remained silent about her rule because Aiden was my friend.

Our family was poor, so we had only visited Watauga Lake on its public shores. My mom couldn't expand on Aiden's statement, so to keep the conversation from turning awkward, she asked me, "What are you going to do about the missing present?"

"I'll call Loila about it later," I lied. "She's staying with her grandparents tonight."

"But I thought—" Aiden started, but a swift look from me closed his mouth. He absent-mindedly wiped cheese dust on the upholstery and stared out the window at the creamsicle sunset.

CHAPTER SIXTEEN

I watched my mom fade. In my eyes, she was a resplendent sunrise, pushing over the mountains and shining light on the day. As each week passed, though, her brilliance lost intensity, slid from its zenith, and approached a sunset of oranges and reds.

Her skin became waxy and pearlescent, drooping from her bones. She didn't have the appetite to eat a lot, so she lost weight. Her disease was finally noticeable to the people around her, and they started to shift pitying looks at my sister and me.

My mom struggled to go to work. She tried to manage the rowdy first graders, but they took too much of her energy. Some days, she could hardly hold her head up on the drive home, so Monique would take us all to school in the morning and drop us off at home in the afternoon. When my mom walked through the door, she shuffled to her bed and laid on it until dinner. Sometimes, she slept. Other times, she stared at her bedroom wall, willing herself to be the woman she was before the disease started eating away her energy, health, and joy.

One night, after cabbage steaks and roasted peppers, my mom and I finally talked about her condition. Lexi was blaring a new gymnastics series in her bedroom, so we sat at the kitchen table, holding hands.

"The doctors said it has spread to my bones," she began.

We didn't need to assign a name to it. The illness that was murdering my mom didn't deserve an identity.

"Start getting the medicine," I begged. "I'll buy you a wig."

"It's not about my hair," she sighed. "I want to be here." She patted the table with her other hand. "I don't want to feel sicker all the time."

"Maybe you could just take it for a little while. You could see if it helped you feel better."

My mom reached out for my other hand. "Razzberry, I want quality time with you and Lexi, not an extended amount of time with an altered consciousness."

"But I heard that there are new drugs that only make you a little sick," I countered. "You're already too tired to do a lot of things anyway—"

My mom recoiled, and her hand slipped away from mine. I had hurt her.

"I'm sorry," I backpedaled. "You're doing a good job, Mom. I only want you to stay with us as long as you can."

"I will," she assured me. "I'll stay here as long as God allows it, but I'll do it naturally."

We were at an impasse. She was unwilling to put anything unnatural into her body, and I wouldn't accept it. I wanted my mom to take drugs that were meant to extend her life, but she wanted to enjoy her life naturally, with very little medical intervention. It was my mom's decision, and there was nothing I could do.

"Now for the hard stuff." A catch in her throat was the only emotion she allowed herself. "When I'm gone, do you want to live with your grandpa?"

I considered the closed-off, unforgiving man. I could handle his drinking binges and late-night shouting at invisible intruders, but Lexi would live in constant fear of his next outburst. I was surprised that my mom had mentioned him as an option.

"He's not good for Lexi," I decided.

"He was much better when I was a girl, but he had my mother there, and she made him happy."

The same disease that was working its way through my mom had plagued my grandmother a decade ago. She had refused to visit the doctor until the choice was taken from her. Part of my mom's decision to stay away from medicine may have been a result of watching her mom go through pain while she was hooked to machines and IVs. I could tell my mom that my grandmother's situation had been different because she waited until the disease had almost completely hijacked her body, but it would have fallen on deaf ears.

"There's always the orphanage," I joked, earning a glare from my mom.

"Would you consider Monique?" she asked timidly.

I thought about her suggestion for a moment, and I realized that there had never been another option. My mom had asked me about my grandfather as a formality, but she had already decided where my sister and I would go after she died.

"She's good to Lexi," I conceded.

"She's good to *you*," my mom returned.

There was a missing package that could challenge my mom's statement, but I blinked my eyes slowly at her remark, neither agreeing nor disagreeing. If Monique was using Scorn, my sister and I wouldn't be safe in her care, but my mom had enough time left to notice the changes if her best friend became addicted to the drug.

"What if something happened to Monique? What if she started using drugs again?"

My mom took a moment to digest my question, rolling around scenarios in her mind. Finally, she said, "She's a healthy woman, but anything can take a life. If she died, maybe it wouldn't happen until you're old enough to care for your sister. Otherwise, there's always Grandpa." She paused and continued with conviction. "As far as drugs go, I think she's through with them. She has a good support group" —she made a circle in the air, indicating the people in our household — "and she takes her recovery seriously."

I nodded my head and hoped the conversation was over. In my eyes, my mom was a superhero, and the disease had seemed like something she could easily defeat. After watching it leave its recent marks on her, I knew that I only had a limited number of days left with my mom.

CHAPTER SEVENTEEN

"Why not?" Lexi whined. "My arm doesn't hurt anymore."

"You have to wear it as long as the doctor tells you so it can heal properly," Monique explained. She demonstrated an arm at an odd angle to show Lexi the possible outcome of removing her cast too soon.

"But it's pink and itchy," Lexi pressed.

Monique rolled her eyes. Lexi had asked her to talk our mom into removing her cast. Her pleas had not worked with our mother, and Monique was even less of a pushover.

I didn't know if my mom had spoken to Monique about her decision to leave us with her when she died, but the possibility made me more nervous around her. I stared out the car window almost the entire way to school. Thankfully, Monique didn't try to engage me in conversation, and my sister was preoccupied with her cast.

The halls of Pale Woods Academy were already moving fluidly when we arrived. Basketball players high-fived and talked about the last game of the season. A banner that advertised the eighth-grade banquet hung loosely on one side. I lifted it up and pressed the tape more firmly to the wall.

"Thank you," spoke a voice. Tabitha had been in the hall behind me, and I realized the banner had been her work. "I couldn't reach it."

Tabitha's petite build allowed her to move freely around the small art studio at school. I had gained two or three inches in the past month, so I was brushing six feet tall.

"I'm sorry about the assembly," I told her.

She glanced away quickly. "It's not your fault. You were only doing what Lieutenant Bane told you to do."

I had the option to brush off the rest of my apology or fix my friendship with Tabitha. I wanted to walk away, but I made myself stand in the hallway and sound as sincere as I felt.

"I saw you were nervous," I fumbled. "I-I should have stopped."

Tabitha was increasingly uncomfortable. She fidgeted with the zipper at the bottom of her jacket.

"I didn't know about—" I paused, trying to find the right way to say what I meant. "I didn't know about your situation until later that day."

"I guess Loila told you," she whispered. She couldn't look at me.

"No, she's not really talking to me anymore," I told her.

Tabitha's head shot up. "Over me?"

"What I did was wrong," I defended. "Loila's just protecting you."

"But I'm not mad at *you*," Tabitha insisted. "Lieutenant Bane knew about my family." She paused before she added, "And your dad."

How did Tabitha know anything about my dad? She hadn't attended Pale Woods Academy until we were in sixth grade. My dad had been gone for six years, and he had disappeared from the town as swiftly as fog lifted when the sun hit the mountains.

"I'll talk to Loila," Tabitha promised, placing a hand on my arm. "I don't want to hurt your chances with her."

My heart skipped a beat. "Huh?" was all I could manage.

Tabitha rolled her eyes and pushed her way through the overcrowded hallway. I barely made it to my first class.

In a few short sentences, Tabitha managed to repair my friendship with Loila. Loila glanced at me, skeptically, but her posture relaxed when Tabitha explained her feelings. I looked at my notebook, like I was studying for the test.

Mr. Fritz passed out our exams, and everyone dipped their heads. All the answers came to me easily, so I was the first one to finish. I stayed in my seat until a couple of people walked their papers to Mr. Fritz's desk.

I chanced a peek at Loila when I passed her seat, and she gave me a half-smile. I tried to keep the corners of my mouth pulled down.

"Do you think Mr. Sams will give me more time on my assignment?" she asked after our first period ended. The question was meant to start an easy conversation so we wouldn't have to discuss our lack of communication since the assembly.

"Yeah," I told her. We both knew Monique would adjust timelines for any student who put forth a positive effort.

"Hey," Aiden called to us.

I was irritated that he had interrupted my conversation with Loila. He knew how awkward things were between us.

"Your sister is busted!" he declared.

I stopped, and several heads turned in our direction. When Aiden saw that he had my attention, he spoke again.

"She paid a guy to saw it off," he said.

"Saw what off?" I asked dumbly.

"Her cast!" he shouted.

The people who passed us walked slowly, picking up as much information as they could gather. I didn't give them a reaction to include in their report.

"Where is she now?" I demanded.

"She's in the office, dude."

I left my friends and hurried down the hall. Monique was standing by her open door, ready to greet me. "Wait! Where are you going?" she called over her shoulder. She tore after me when she received no response, but I was faster than her, so I was already in the office when she caught up to me.

The receptionist, Mrs. Jackson, was expecting me. "Go on in, Mr. Krovopuskov," she said. "Your mother thought you might show up."

I rolled my fingers over the wooden door to announce myself before I opened it. My sister and mom sat in chairs across from Principal Bailey. She beckoned me inside, but she couldn't offer me a chair.

Lexi appeared smug, and my mom held onto a chair for support. I stood in the corner behind my sister.

"I was just asking Lexi why she wanted her cast off," Principal Bailey informed me.

"And I was about to say that I was done wearing it, and it was itchy," Lexi replied. She threw me a backwards glance, assuming my usual apathetic attitude indicated support for her rebellion.

"That was dumb," I said.

Everyone looked at me with surprise. Lexi cocked her head and narrowed her eyes.

"It's *my* choice," she asserted. "*I'm* the one who has to wear it."

"You didn't think of anyone else," I countered. "Now, Mom has to leave work early to take you back to the doctor and get another cast put on your arm."

"I'm not wearing another cast," Lexi sassed.

My mom was too weak to argue, so I took over. "You'll go to the doctor, and you'll wear the cast. Do you think your arm will stay in the right place without it?"

"But my arm is fine!" She made a show of moving it erratically. My mom and Principal Bailey winced.

"It may be fine today," Principal Bailey said, "but it can grow at an odd angle if you don't keep it in the cast." She smiled at my sister. "It's been two weeks, so you should only have four more weeks to go."

We were able to get my sister to go the doctor, but she made a compromise for me to go with her. Principal Bailey excused me from classes for the rest of the day so I could help my mom with my sister. She tried not to look when I steadied my mom as she got out of her chair.

"Where is Mr. Sams?" I asked when we passed the receptionist.

"She went back to class when she saw you go into Principal Bailey's office," Mrs. Jackson explained.

After a quick stop in my mom's classroom, we packed into the car, and drove to Johnson City. My mom didn't speak. She was upset about missing over half a day's pay.

The orthopedic doctor couldn't see Lexi, and they instructed us to go to the emergency room. We waited for over two hours before we were finally placed in a room. My mom continued to pale, so I went to the vending machines and got her a soda and a pack of crackers. My mom huffed when I brought Lexi the same lunch.

"It's all they had."

"They had decaffeinated soda," my mom remarked.

"The button wouldn't work," I lied, and winked at Lexi. She turned her head, still mad at me for helping our mom take her to the hospital.

The doctor rushed in, told us about x-rays and compromised healing, and admonished Lexi for taking off her cast. "This will be another co-pay for your mother," he informed her, "so you may want to think of that before you ask a little boy to saw off another cast."

Lexi pursed her lips. "He's not a little boy. He's the same age as my brother."

I made a mental note to find the boy and talk to him. Or punch him.

A nurse transported Lexi for her x-ray. She looked a little more defeated when she returned.

"I'm sorry, Mom," she said sincerely. "I was miserable in that cast, and I really felt good enough for it to come off."

Our mom patted Lexi's leg. She didn't say anything, but everything seemed like an effort for her. My mom was in pain, but she wouldn't share her physical ailments with us. I resolved to let her have her pride. Besides, once the disease passed a certain point, she wouldn't feel like she had a lot of dignity.

I paced the room for an hour. The nurse checked on my sister and gave her a remote that controlled the television, so Lexi happily flipped through the available options. My mom fell asleep in her chair. Her arm slipped a little off the arm rest, and I was able to adjust her so that she didn't fall onto the floor.

We jerked to attention when the doctor rapped lightly on the door. He entered, still looking at my sister's chart. For a moment, when he glanced up, he moved his eyes from my mom to my sister, as if he couldn't determine which one was in need of his care. I couldn't blame him. My mom's short nap had robbed her of any vitality.

He tapped the chart, "It looks good," he announced. He crossed the distance to my sister's bedside, and gently moved her arm in different directions. He stood between my sister and me, so I couldn't read his expression as he examined her. "Where does it hurt?"

"Nowhere," Lexi answered.

The doctor paused his exam. "Why did you visit the ER today?"

My mom and I exchanged a glance. Hadn't the same doctor just seen Lexi a couple of hours ago? Maybe it had been a hard day and he had attended to a lot of patients.

"I paid a boy to cut off my cast early," my sister answered honestly.

The doctor closed his posture and lectured, "You should have let the doctor remove your cast. Do you realize that you could have been cut by the tool the boy used?"

"I wanted it off me. It was itchy."

"That's a common complaint," the doctor validated.

"Excuse me, doctor," my mom interrupted. "When will she receive her new cast?"

The doctor tapped the chart again and referenced the x-rays inside it. "I see no need to put her in another cast."

"Will her bones heal correctly?' my mom questioned.

"When was her cast scheduled to come off?"

"In a little over a month," my mom returned.

The doctor appeared puzzled. "How long has she worn it?"

"Almost two weeks," my sister answered.

The doctor studied her arm again, moving it in various angles. "You're a fast healer," he surmised. "Be happy that you aren't like most of the kids that have to wear a cast for a couple of months."

My sister shined a self-satisfied smile at our mom.

"You may want to follow up with your orthopedic doctor, but you're free to go home today," the doctor told us.

"Do some people heal faster than others?" my sister asked.

In his mind, the doctor had already moved on to the next patient, but he backtracked when he heard my sister's question. "The short answer is yes. The guidelines for medicine apply to the way a majority of people have responded to a particular treatment. Most people need six to eight weeks to heal with the type of injury you had. But there are some people who need longer, and there are people like you, who don't need as much time."

"Is it weird that I healed so fast?"

The doctor smiled. "It's a little out of the ordinary, but it's nothing to put in the Guinness Book of World Records."

In the car, Lexi used her arm for everything. She rested on it, waved at passing cars, and moved it to the music in her mind.

"Hey, Mom," she called from the backseat. Our mom raised her eyebrows at her in the rearview mirror. "Can I have an ice cream, since I saved you money on a new cast?"

Our mom's eyebrows climbed higher. "You also racked up an emergency room bill," she replied. "By the time the expenses for the radiology, doctor, and room are broken down and paid, it will cost more than the appointment we had for the orthopedic specialist."

Lexi's chipper disposition wavered, but it didn't disappear. She made a game of waving one side of her hand to a vehicle, and then the other side to the next car.

Our mom napped all afternoon, and Lexi sulked in her room. She hadn't realized that she would still be grounded, even though she didn't need the cast anymore.

I shoved my hand under my mattress and pulled out two twenties the neighbors had given me for helping them remove dead limbs from a tree. They had been surprised by my dexterity and strength when I had leapt easily from the branches and carried them to the roadside. I hoped the amount would go undetected and placed it in my mom's wallet. It wasn't enough to pay for the emergency room visit, but maybe my mom could buy lunch for herself for the rest of the week.

I made a meatless dinner, and my mom ate it gratefully when she woke up from her nap. Lexi sighed and huffed, but no one spoke.

I spent the rest of the night in my room. I finished the homework my teachers had sent to me in less than an hour, so I answered some of the messages from Loila and Aiden.

A light tap on the door mimicked my rolling knock. My sister opened my door and pushed it shut. She sat on my bed and stared at me. I stared back, waiting for her to speak.

"My father healed fast, didn't he?" Lexi asked. She had been very small when he had left our family, so she had no reason to reference him by more than a convenient title.

"Yeah," I answered.

"It hurts Mom when we have things that are like him, doesn't it?"

I rolled her question around. I hadn't really paid attention to it at the time, but my mom had seemed more contemplative at dinner. "It's just hard for her because she loved him. She's able to let it go when she's not thinking about him, but things like my eyes, and what happened with you today, remind her of him. It just reopens the wound."

Lexi nodded. "Is it bad that I don't care about what happened to him?"

"You don't remember him," I said, shrugging. "How can you care about someone you didn't know?"

Lexi stared at the floor for a long time before she stood up to leave. "Well, at least I got one good thing from him."

I wondered if I could say the same.

CHAPTER EIGHTEEN

The bruise was on his chin. It bobbed up and down when he spoke, stretching to appear more on his cheek one moment and sliding just under his jawbone the next. He didn't try to cover it. He laughed and joked like he didn't have the compliments of the bruise dotting his wrists. I saw them when his shirt pulled tight from stretching or using his hands when he spoke.

I let him do all the talking, but between his forced merriment and witty remarks, I hoped he would let me know how I could help him.

"What happened to your chin?" Monique asked him when she greeted us at the door.

"I punched myself when I pulled up my blanket," Aiden laughed, mimicking the action.

Monique noticed the matching bruises on his wrists. She and I shared a quick look. Monique couldn't call out Aiden for his lie, but I was grateful to have an adult see the marks on my friend.

"You must have a tough jaw to have bruised both your wrists too," Monique remarked.

Aiden stopped laughing.

When we sat down, Aiden said, "I like Mr. Sams, but sometimes she needs to mind her own business."

I didn't respond. I thought Monique spoke out whenever it was necessary, and I agreed with her assessment.

By lunch, Loila had noticed Aiden's bruised chin, and she was giving me pointed stares. I avoided her gaze.

"What's on your chin?" Tabitha asked Aiden.

"I was half-asleep, and I caught it on my dresser," he replied.

Tabitha smiled, but it didn't reach her eyes. She knew he was lying. She had lived with an aggressive father and a mother who told stories to explain away the marks he had given her.

My ears perked up at his new reason. I had been with Aiden when he had told Monique about punching himself in the face while pulling up his blanket. *Did he want me to realize that he was lying without telling me the truth? Did he want me to intervene without asking for help?*

Loila looked from me to Aiden's wrists. She urged me to acknowledge what I already knew. I nodded almost imperceptibly.

After school, I asked Aiden if he wanted to go to the cave.

"I've got ball practice," he said. "Do you want to come with me?"

"Nah." The bruises were evidence that his father was back in town, and I didn't really want to hear him shout at my friend about his shortcomings on the baseball field. "Loila and Tabitha are supposed to be going to the cave."

Aiden smiled knowingly. "Okay, Romeo," he chuckled.

I smiled sadly, and he pretended not to notice. Why was it seen as a weakness for Aiden to admit that he was physically abused? Had his father threatened him against revealing that part of their homelife, or was Aiden embarrassed that his financial status wouldn't protect him from domestic violence? I wanted to take him home with me and keep him safe from whatever waited for him at home, but I could only watch him walk away with his mitt rolled into his hand.

***

"Can't he tell someone?" Loila asked.

"His father is rich," Tabitha said. "He can cover it up."

"But Mr. Sams saw it," Loila argued. "He can't go against the word of a teacher."

"She has a past," I told them. "He can bring it up to destroy her credibility."

"If she's good enough to be a teacher then her statement about the marks on Aiden should be enough evidence," Loila pressed.

"I agree with you," Tabitha countered. "But money will make anything go away. He can even pay people to be false witnesses."

"So Aiden has to keep living in abuse?" Loila shouted.

I paced the width of the cave slowly. Tabitha looked at her feet.

Loila threw up her hands, and she knocked her pen off her notepad. "What has to happen to get Aiden out of the situation?"

I was good at remaining stoic, no matter my true feelings. I picked up her pen and placed it on her notepad.

"His father will have to kill him, or come close to it," Tabitha spoke miserably.

In that moment, I knew that Tabitha had experienced a similar situation. Loila understood it, too.

"Your dad was abusive before..." Loila trailed off, purposely omitting the murder.

"Yeah. He would hurt my mom when he got upset, or when she tried to protect me. He grabbed her arms, or tried to strangle her, so she wore long sleeved shirts and scarves."

"I was little, but I thought her scarves were pretty," Loila commented.

Tabitha smiled. "Yeah. I always liked the one with the orange butterflies.

"They were monarchs," I said, surprising myself. I hadn't known that the memory of Tabitha's mother's scarves was so strong until she mentioned it. "She wore them all the time."

"She had to." Tabitha shrugged her shoulders.

Loila sensed a need to shift the conversation. "What are we going to do about Aiden?"

"What about me?" Aiden asked, rounding the entrance to the cave. He had changed out of his baseball uniform, but he had the smell of dirt and fresh grass stains.

We all panicked. I searched for a reasonable response, but I couldn't find one. Loila and Tabitha were looking at me for help.

He laughed. "C'mon on. My birthday's not for a couple of months, and I already have a party planned. It's no surprise."

I tried to smile and pretend nothing was going on. Aiden wouldn't let it drop.

"What is it?" he pressed. "What are you going to do about me?"

Loila walked across the length of the cave and burst into tears. She slung her arms around Aiden, and he hugged her automatically. *What did I do?* he mouthed to me.

Tabitha used his surprise to our advantage. *Take it easy on her,* she mouthed.

Aiden patted Loila's back, bewildered. Everything may have been fine if Loila had known that her tears had solved the situation. Instead, she made it worse.

"I don't want him to hurt you anymore," she whimpered.

Aiden moved her to arm's length. He stared at her hard. "What do you mean?"

Loila gestured at Tabitha and me. "We all know."

"What do you know?" Aiden seethed. He dropped his hands from Loila's arms.

"Your dad is hurting you," she cried. "We want to help you."

Aiden locked eyes with me. I felt like I had betrayed him, even though he hadn't shared the truth with me.

"Is this some sort of intervention?" he barked. "I told you that I fell up the steps!" He had told so many lies about his father's abuse that he couldn't remember which one he had told us.

I could see we weren't going to be able to help him or make him feel any better about his circumstances. "It's okay, man. We don't have to talk about it."

Loila took Aiden's hand. "Yes we do. This is your safe place, Aiden." She nodded to Tabitha and me. "We are all friends here, and we want to help you." She turned back to Aiden. "Don't you want to get away before he kills you?"

Aiden untangled his hand. "What are you talking about?" he yelled. "My dad would never kill me." He grabbed his chin unconsciously. "You guys know me?" he added fiercely. "Well, then you know that I can be rude and sarcastic. My dad travels around the world, and he knows people who would be offended by the things I say. A little knock around the dinner table is nothing compared to what would happen to me if I said the wrong things in the wrong places."

"I say the wrong things sometimes," Tabitha volunteered. "My uncle just tells me why they're wrong and not to say them again."

"But you're a girl," Aiden dismissed. "And your uncle's only a manager in a supermarket. How far are you gonna go? He's never going to own a chain of stores, so you're probably going to stay in Erwin your whole life. It won't matter what you say."

Tabitha's fingers curled into fits, and she shot up. Her face was inches away from Aiden's. They both breathed in angry puffs.

"You just said something terrible to me," Tabitha snapped. "But I'm not going to hit you." She took a couple of enraged breaths, her eyes never dropping from Aiden's stare. "Your dad may have a lot of money and he might travel all over the world, but he will *never* be as good as my uncle."

Aiden couldn't find words strong enough for her before Tabitha stormed out of the cave. Loila and I couldn't think of a way to diffuse the situation. After an uncomfortable moment, Aiden stomped off around the opposite side of the cave.

Loila threw her hands up at me. "You were no help at all!" she said. She slung her notebook on the rock where she kept it. *"It's okay, man,"* she mocked. *"We don't have to talk about it."* She extended the mimicry of my voice and put words in my mouth. *"I'm just going to watch your father beat you until you die."*

"Hey," I warned.

"Well, what do you think is going to happen? Do you think Aiden will ever be as polished as his father wants?"

I didn't think he would be the son his father envisioned, but it was hard for me to see Aiden's father murdering him. I related my thoughts to Loila.

"Okay," she said. "So maybe he doesn't kill Aiden. What kind of life is it for him to live?"

I shrugged. I felt like it wasn't my business, but Loila insisted that we needed to be involved.

"We're going to have to do it another way," I suggested. "He wants to defend his father, so we have to make him see that it's not the way a family operates."

"That's perfect!" Loila said. "I know how you can start."

"What?" I didn't know that she had been depending on me to carry out my suggestion.

"The next time his father leaves, invite him to stay with your family," she explained. "He'll see how a real family solves conflicts."

"He spends the night sometimes," I offered, unwilling to share my space for an extended period of time.

"Sure," she hedged. "But let him see the way your family handles stuff every day. My mom gets upset over towels in the bathroom floor, but when Tabitha spends the night, my mom just picks up the towels and says something to me after she goes home. But if Tabitha was spending a week with us, my mom would tell me to pick them up."

I understood the difference, but my family was in a different situation than the one at Loila's house. I reminded her about my mom's diagnosis.

"I don't want to make you mad, Razz, but it's better for Aiden to see that your mom handles the things you and Lexi do without violence, even though she's sick."

I didn't like to talk about my mom's illness. It made it too real for me, and the day when I would have to be without her seemed to be approaching faster than I had guessed. I tried to lighten the conversation with humor.

"Aiden should have been there when Lexi cut off her cast," I commented. "He would have really seen how my mom keeps her temper in check!"

Loila laughed, and her dimples lifted. I tried to limit the time I smiled at her, so she wouldn't suspect my feelings.

"Did she cut it off herself?"

"No," I replied. "She paid someone in our class."

"Who would have done that?" Loila said. "She's only in second grade."

"Aiden said that it was probably Evan," I told her.

"Oh."

Loila and I had gone to school with Evan since the sixth grade. He had been at a public school, but he transferred into Pale Woods Academy when his sister was recruited. He didn't have her intelligence, but Principal Bailey liked to keep siblings at the same school. Evan's technical skills were top notch, so he used them to gain status with his classmates. Sometimes he crossed a line, though, like he did when he cut off my sister's cast.

"I'm going to talk to him about it."

"That sounds like a fun conversation," she chuckled.

"I'll fight him if I have too," I said, straightening my posture.

Loila looked away from me, and I thought I saw her roll her eyes. "I don't think Evan is going to want to fight you," she said. "He just saw a chance to make some money."

Neither one of us spoke for a while. I paced, and Loila picked at a fingernail.

"Are you going to the banquet?" she asked.

My breath caught in my throat. "I've not really thought about it," I lied.

"Well, I've thought about it. I've thought about it a lot." She locked eyes with me.

For the first time, I wondered if I had a chance with Loila. Part of me had thought of her as beyond my reach.

My phone buzzed audibly in my pocket, saving me from embarrassment. I dove into my pocket and told Loila that a spammy text was my mom telling me to go home.

Loila stopped me on my way out, her hand sending tingles up my arm. "I hope you go to the banquet. And if you go, wear a black suit. Black really brings out the gold in your eyes."

It was still daylight when I started home, but I felt someone following me. I slowed my pace, and I could almost feel the vibrations of their feet, even though they kept a good distance from me.

I walked into a gas station to give them time to reveal themselves or stop following me. I was surprised when a tall man, dressed completely in black stooped through the door. He made no attempt to disguise his interest in me, so I stayed within sight of the attendant.

I picked up a cup and filled it with varying amounts of each soda. My father had called it a "suicide drink."

"Have you noticed a difference yet?" a voice asked.

I startled, and I almost spilled the contents of my cup. I kept my back to him, pretending that I didn't hear him.

The man sighed heavily. "Okay, kid, if you want to talk to someone who knows what it's like, I think you know where you can find me."

I heard the door jingle when he left. I walked up to the counter to pay for my drink.

"Are you okay?" the attendant asked.

"Yeah, it was just some creeper," I reassured her.

I walked the rest of the way home without the feeling I was being followed. The man had said what he had wanted to say and returned to wherever he went.

How was I supposed to know where to find him?

My mind supplied me with the only reasonable answer. He had been one of the guards at the abandoned plant.

He probably thought I was going through withdrawals since I had only taken the vial his boss had thrown in my direction. Maybe he sold Scorn and wanted to see if the drug had increased my speed or strength. He wouldn't know my science teacher had taken it from my hiding place.

I had been afraid to go back to the plant to steal more Scorn, but he had practically invited me. If he thought I was a buyer then maybe I could find a way to pretend that I wanted to purchase some, back out at the last minute, and steal a vial of Scorn. Monique had taken my Scorn, so it was the only hope I had of testing the drug's effectiveness.

I decided that I would take him up on his offer, but I couldn't do it alone.

CHAPTER NINETEEN

I discovered the puff of hair in the shower. My mom had given me a book that told me that hair could appear overnight, but I had hoped that it would be the same amount under both arms. However, it was unequally weighted. My right arm had a few strings of black hair, but there was a downy puff of hair under my left arm.

I made the mistake of showing my mom the difference. She looked at me strangely before she adopted a careless attitude.

"You know that hormones can make your body do all kinds of weird and beautiful things," she started.

I stopped her lecture. "It's all good, Mom," I chuckled. "I just wanted to show you."

"Well, thank you for sharing it with me," she responded.

I walked away before it was even more awkward. My mom was great with little kids, but teenagers were unexplored territory for her. That's why she bought me the book. She wanted to be a caring parent, but she had no idea how to respond to certain situations.

I thought about shaving it, but I didn't have enough time to hop back into the shower before Monique picked me up from school. I rolled deodorant over the hair and hoped that it wouldn't make me sweat too much.

Lexi was just finishing her cereal when I strutted into the kitchen. She wore a yellow top and red skirt with rainbow tights and arm sleeves that extended to wrap around the bottom of her thumb.

"If you carried a piece of fruit with you then you could advertise computers," I teased.

Lexi rolled her eyes. "That company changed their name years ago. I'm trying out for a part in the school play," she informed me. "I want to be noticed."

I pretended to shield my eyes. Lexi swatted at me and missed.

Our mom breezed past us on the way to the door, stuffing pens and tissues into her ancient handbag. "Are you guys ready?" she asked. "I'm teaching borrowing today, and I have to get the number blocks out of my storage closet."

"Where's Monique?" I asked.

"I think she's having feminine trouble," my mom replied. "It hits her pretty hard every month."

"Seriously, Mom? You couldn't just say that she was taking a sick day?"

My mom sighed. "It's a natural process. It shouldn't upset you to talk about it."

"It's not a natural process for me," I countered.

"But you have a sister."

I understood the reason for my mom's emphasis. At the rate her illness was progressing, she probably wouldn't be around when my sister made her jump into womanhood. Lexi would have Monique, but she needed to be aware that she could talk about her changes with me.

Lexi bounced to the car, and I put my arm around my mom's shoulder. She made a small noise when she smelled my hefty deodorant. Heavy scents upset her stomach. I tried to pull my arm away, but she grabbed my hand and leaned against me.

"You're my favorite boy, Razzberry."

"I'm your *only* boy," I laughed.

"Do you want to drive?" my mom asked suddenly.

I was completely thrown off guard. I had only sat idly in the passenger seat. I hadn't thought about the mechanics of driving because I couldn't get my permit for another fourteen months.

"Sure," I responded carefully.

My mom sensed my hesitation. "It's okay," she encouraged. "The car's an automatic, so all you have to do is steer, brake, and go."

She listed the operations nonchalantly, but I was certain there was much more to driving a vehicle that weighed over a ton. I was glad that I had put on extra deodorant.

"What is he doing?" Lexi asked when I hopped into the driver's seat.

"He's going to die," my mom spoke, and corrected herself by saying "drive," but not before my sister latched onto her mistake.

"We're all going to *die*," she laughed.

My mom helped me navigate the two roads that took us to Pale Woods Academy. I found out early that I applied too much pressure to the break. I almost came to a full stop fifty feet away from a red light.

"You have to tap the break sometimes," my mom instructed.

I drove speedily around curves, due to my reluctance to touch the break. My mom and Lexi hung onto the arm rests on their car doors. My sister made little shrieks around each curve, and my mom sucked in her breath. I thought I saw her trying to push an imaginary break on her side of the car.

The turn into the school's parking lot loomed in front of me, challenging the limits of my cool. My inexperience made me increasingly irritated, but I managed not to snap at my mom when she chanted, "Just tap the break."

I slowed the car, and a vehicle approached behind me. It would run into me if I braked too suddenly.

I pressed my foot on the break, and almost jerked us to a stop. The vehicle behind us lurched. Lexi glanced behind her, and yelled, "We're all gonna die!"

My mom shushed her while maintaining her chant.

I slung the car into the parking lot, and almost hit an SUV. The driver stared at me in wide-eyed shock.

My mom usually parked in the teacher's section, but she raised no objection when I guided the car into a parking space in the last row of the visitor's lot.

Lexi jumped out of the car and fell on her knees, pretending to kiss the ground. "I'm alive," she shouted dramatically.

My mom was even paler than usual, and she accepted her car keys with a shaky hand. "That was good for your first time behind the wheel," she said.

"Stop your theatrics," my mom warned my sister when we got out of the car.

Aiden caught up to my family at the walk that led to the main school building. My mom and Lexi broke apart from Aiden and me, giving us time to talk.

"Were you driving, bro?" Aiden asked me.

"Yeah," I answered casually.

"I didn't think you got your permit until next year."

"I don't," I told him. When he seemed puzzled, I said, "My mom's sick, so she's doing things with Lexi and me in case something happens."

"That's tough," he sighed.

I was glad that he was talking to me, and he didn't make a joke about my mom's attempt to complete a family bucket list with us before she passed.

"Hey, did your dad leave for China yesterday?" I asked.

"Stop, dude," he warned.

I held my hands up. "No, that's not what I mean. I only wanted to see if you wanted to hang out at my house until he got back."

Aiden thought it over. "Yeah, I could come crash at your house for a while."

Rowan stopped us in the hallway. "I'm running for student body vice-president. Can I count on your vote?"

Aiden examined her almond eyes and dark hair and quickly agreed. I was a little more skeptical.

"I don't know you. Why would I vote for you?" I motioned to a poster of another candidate on the wall. "Seth's running too, and he's been on the student council since he was old enough to join."

"You're right," she replied, surprising Aiden and me. "You should vote for the candidate you believe has the most experience." She smiled slyly. "But I created the student council at my last school."

"That's cool," Aiden said. He crossed his arms to show the budding muscles in his arms.

Rowan ignored him and spoke to me. "I organized a fundraiser that helped every club in the school. I planted trees and cleaned the pond every month."

"You did all that by yourself," I quipped.

"I think you know very well that I was only the moving force behind it, but I did get my hands dirty," she returned smartly. "I dug the holes for the trees, and I skimmed dead leaves and fish out of the pond."

"A regular Mother Theresa," Aiden interjected.

Rowan and I stared at him. "Mother Theresa cared for sick people," I reminded him.

Rowan moved down the hall to pass out more flyers, but not before she touched my arm. I avoided her eyes, but I could feel her stare.

"She likes you," Aiden observed. He put his arms down and knit his eyebrows together. "She's trouble."

"I know," I responded to both of his statements.

———◇———

My mom solved our usual dinner dilemma by making pizza. She used a cauliflower crust, and Aiden chewed noisily.

"Do you like your food, Aiden?" my mom asked.

"Yes, Mrs. K." he responded around a mouthful of food. "But I usually eat pizza with pepperoni and bacon."

My head shot up from over my plate. I had expected my mom to give Aiden the same talk that she had given me about her vegetarian choices, but she only said, "We don't eat meat here anymore."

The conversation would have ended, but Aiden asked, "Why? Is it because your husband was eaten?"

I coughed out a bite of pizza. Lexi dropped her fork noisily onto her plate. My mom stared at him, her face unreadable.

Aiden didn't realize the impact of his question, but he understood that the emotional temperature in the room had dropped a couple of degrees. He stared from one of us to the next, waiting on an answer.

Finally, I spoke. "We don't talk about it."

I thought my statement would break the tension, or relieve some of the pressure on my mom to answer, but Aiden asked, "Why don't you talk about it? Don't you miss him?"

"He left us before he died," my sister explained flatly. "I don't care if the bear ate him whole!"

Aiden missed my sister's rising emotions. "It didn't, did it?"

"I don't know!" Lexi shot back at him. "I'm just a kid!"

She ran off to her room. I couldn't tell if she was going to cry or scream and kick the walls.

Aiden crunched another bite of his pizza as if he hadn't done anything to precipitate Lexi's outburst. When my mom spoke, it was kind and gentle.

"Aiden, what happened to Razz's father is not the reason the people in this house are vegetarians," she began. "Razz, Lexi, and I don't like the unfair treatment of animals in the meat market." She added, "Gregori was kind and gentle with his family, but he chased fame and fortune."

"By fighting bears?" Aiden remarked.

My mom took a shaky breath and pushed down her anger. When she answered my friend, it was with an even tone. "He liked to camp in the woods. He just happened to camp near a bear's den."

"Oh," Aiden said. "Can I have more parmesan cheese?"

Aiden was oblivious to the trouble he had caused. My mom graciously passed him the cheese.

"Cheese comes from animals," he expressed. "Why do you eat it?" He raised his eyebrows as if he had caught my mom in a fine point.

My mom blinked her eyes slowly and widened her smile. "Aiden," she sighed. "We aren't vegan. Vegans don't eat meat or animal products, but vegetarians eat everything except meat and sometimes eggs, depending on their beliefs."

Aiden nodded his head while he processed my mom's words. "Sure, but if you're going to be vegetarians, then why aren't you vegans? It just seems like being a vegetarian is only doing it halfway."

Color flooded my mom's neck and face. "I'll certainly consider that," she said deliberately.

Aiden finished his pizza and pushed back from the table. I took both our plates when he didn't make a move to carry his dish to the sink.

I placed my hand on my mom's shoulder briefly to show her my appreciation for keeping her cool with my friend. She had shown restraint, so it had been a good example for Aiden, but he hadn't understood the full situation. He had no idea that he had crossed a line. Several times.

My mom patted my hand and told me to go with Aiden. I didn't want her to stand and wash the dishes, but she insisted.

Aiden moved around my room, looking at the pictures my mom had put of Lexi and me on the wall. "I wish I had a brother or sister," he said.

"Yeah, Lexi's pretty great," I admitted. "When she's not jumping on me or kicking the walls."

We both chuckled. I grabbed my phone and plopped onto my bed.

Aiden laid on his back and rested his arm behind his head. He stared at the ceiling for a long time. "Did you see him after it happened?" he asked.

"What?"

Aiden turned on his side and looked at me. "Your dad," he clarified. "Did you see what the bear did to him?"

His question sparked a memory that I didn't want to relive. "No," I lied. "I was with my mom when it happened."

He turned back onto his back. "I wonder what it was like," he said. "Do you think he tried to fight it?"

"It's human instinct to want to preserve your life." I tried to sound nonchalant, but my friend's questions were irritating me.

Five short rhythmic raps were followed by two even shorter knocks. My mom peeked into the room. "Do you boys need anything before I go to bed?"

We both shook our heads.

"What was that knock you did?" Aiden asked.

"Oh, my dad used to do it all the time," my mom explained. "It's shave and a haircut, two bits," she sang.

Aiden snarled his nose. "My dad just knocks."

My mom's extra wide smile returned, the one she usually reserved for troublesome first graders. "Well, you boys have a good night," she said sweetly. "I love you, Razzberry."

"Razzberry," Aiden laughed when she closed the door. "That's priceless. Wait till Loila hears—"

"Shut up!" I barked before I could stop myself. It was unlike me to lash out, and Aiden was shocked. It took a moment for his defenses to go up, but his face fell from jovial to concerned to angry as I spoke. I could hardly recall everything I spat at him, but I remembered telling him, "You walk around putting people down, just because you have money. Well, guess what? It doesn't make you cool, it makes you a—"

Aiden slammed the door on my last word, but I still meant it. I had been fuming since dinner, but I had wanted my home life to be a good example for him. I had ruined all my mom's efforts to show kindness to my entitled friend.

I slung the pillows off the bed. They struck the wall harmlessly. I paced the room, ready to knock off everything on the dresser and rip pictures off the walls. *Why did I feel this way?* I knew the right thing to do, and I usually didn't feel upset.

It made me even angrier to think about what my mom would say about my outburst, especially after I had shown her the huge puff of hair under one of my arms. She would tell me that my hormones were responsible for my feelings, and it was all natural. I really didn't want to hear that I was unused to the surge of testosterone that I was feeling. *I wanted to be upset!* Aiden was rude, and someone had to put him in check.

I bolted out my door in a fury. Heat and rage radiated from my skin. I stopped abruptly in the hallway.

Aiden was slumped against the hall wall with his head in his hands. Lexi and my mom stood over him, soothing him with soft words. My mom sat down on the floor and placed one arm around him, still speaking soothing words into his ear. My sister put her arm on his shoulder, unclear about the best way to help him.

At first, I was infuriated. *How could my mom and Lexi comfort Aiden after he had been so thoughtless!* But then I heard him sobbing, and I made out snatches of the conversation.

"...and it doesn't matter that I don't like her."

"Have you tried to talk to anyone about it?"

"It wouldn't matter. He would just pay them to act like it was a lie."

"Your dad couldn't shut me up," my sister voiced defiantly. She had finally found a way to contribute to the situation, and it fit her eight-year-old sense of justice. "He's a bully, and bully's go to jail."

Aiden looked up at her, his face ringed with sweat and tears. "No, you don't get it," he reiterated. "He won't go to jail. He will just pay the judge to say that your family is crazy, or make it seem like you were after his money."

"But you have burn marks on your ankles," Lexi argued.

Aiden instinctively pushed his sleeves down. My mom glared at Lexi.

"It's past your bedtime," she told my sister.

Lexi stared at our mom intently, gesturing to Aiden's obvious breakdown. She thought that she was helping more with her honesty than with her silence.

"Go to your room," my mom insisted.

After an overexaggerated huff, Lexi marched off. She rolled her eyes at me, upset with me for causing the situation and angry at our mom for dismissing her.

Aiden noticed me. I crossed the distance between us and sat beside him, my back against the wall and my forearms resting on the tops of my knees.

He wiped his eyes, and my mom got him tissues and a bottle of water. She and I sat with him, waiting for him to speak.

"Is it weird that I still love him?" Aiden asked us.

"No," my mom replied. "I had a friend in college who stayed with her abusive boyfriend because she loved him, and she thought he loved her."

Aiden's posture stiffened. "But he's not my boyfriend! He's my father! Shouldn't he love and protect me?"

"Yes," my mom agreed, "but people who love you don't burn you." She motioned to his ankles.

I had picked up something small from their conversation and the talk I'd had with my mom about Aiden's mother. I voiced it carefully.

"His dad isn't burning him. His mother did."

"Savannah burned you?" my mom said, aghast.

Aiden wouldn't comment. He took a long drink of his water and stared at the opposite wall.

"She smoked cigarettes," my mom realized, making the connection to the type of burns on my friend's legs.

Aiden had reached the end of sharing and he closed himself off. My mom tried to open him back up, but he was finished with revealing the nature of his household with us.

I understood the need for his humor and careless words. It was an act he kept up to prevent people from thinking that he was like either one of his parents.

"Hey, do you want to go watch a movie?" I asked.

Aiden, my mom, and I rose together. My mom kept eyeballing my friend like she expected him to fall.

After my outburst, I thought that I might wait a couple of days before I asked Aiden to go with me to the abandoned factory, but as I sat in the room with him, it seemed clearer to me that my friend needed a distraction.

"Hey," I called over to him.

He had piled blankets and pillows around him, cushioning himself against the carpeted floor. He looked up at me.

"Do you want to lay around like the princess and the pea all night, or do you want to go to the abandoned factory?"

"What's there?" he asked skeptically.

"Scorn."

Color rose from his chest to his neck. "So, you do drugs now?"

I explained my reasons to him, and he seemed to understand. "How do you know it's there?"

"I heard a kid talking about it," I lied.

Aiden rolled it around in his mind, but he finally agreed to go with me. We waited until we thought my mom and Lexi were asleep, and we slipped silently through the window.

CHAPTER TWENTY

We rounded the corner with the full moonlight casting shadows on familiar places. Neighborhood dogs barked their disapproval at our late-night excursion.

"Do you wear contacts?" Aiden asked me when we were far enough away from my house.

"No," I told him. "My mom wears contacts, but she said Lexi and I have perfect vision."

He kept moving his face to get a better look at my eyes, and it started to make me feel uncomfortable. I wished that I could close my eyes so that he wouldn't try to stare at me so intently.

"I'm not your type," I joked.

Aiden dismissed my jab. "They're really gold."

"My mom says it's hormones," I said nervously, embarrassing us both. Guys didn't talk about puberty.

"Did you braid each other's hair and talk about your feelings?" he teased.

"No, but your dad told my mom that Midol helped with his period pain."

"I wish he'd take one, then, and get off my case," Aiden laughed.

Humor was my friend's way of dealing with anything that made him uncomfortable. Part of me had always known it, but I didn't think of it as his coping mechanism until our recent argument.

We ducked behind trees and bushes when we saw headlights. A police car glided past us, and we concocted a short-lived idea that my mom had heard our plans through the bedroom door, called the police, and we were caught. I knew that my mom was asleep, though. It was hard for her to stay awake.

The abandoned factory was bathed in moonlight. It was still and silent, like the houses that faced it. We stood across from it, shielded by the shadows of proud, two-story homes.

"Do you think someone is in there?" Aiden whispered.

"Yeah. They wouldn't leave Scorn unguarded."

"But why is it in Erwin?" he asked. "They can't really sell it to a lot of people here."

"It's a good place. No one really goes on that property, it's a quick drive to the interstate, and the hill behind it is covered in trees."

"Why does the hill matter?"

"Because anyone inside has a chance of escaping by hiding in the trees."

Aiden nodded. "So, what's the plan?"

"I'll go inside and get the Scorn, and you stay outside and let me know if someone is coming to the building."

"I want to go in too," Aiden argued.

"Then who will go get help if I need it?"

"I'll run and get the police if you get caught," Aiden promised.

"How can you run if we're both caught?" I pointed out.

Aiden realized that he couldn't argue with me, but he tried anyway. "What if I get caught while you're inside? I'm a sitting duck."

The moonlight was bright, but there was a shadowed area just beyond the building and the dumpster. The broken window that I'd gained access through the last time was just above the dumpster. I directed my friend to the darkness, and we bolted across the street.

I found proper footing on the damaged dumpster, and I scurried up it and into the window, avoiding the small shards that still stuck up along the frame. I heard a noise and thrust my head outside. I drew a line across my throat in Aiden's direction to indicate that his silence was necessary. He whispered something, but I ducked into the dark building.

I felt my way along the wide beams that ran around the factory. One beam had collapsed, and I slid down it. My boots hit the floor undetected. There was a repetitive noise in another room that muffled most small sounds. I carefully stepped around discarded soda bottles and collected dust piles until I entered an area that was clean and disinfected. Lemon smells replaced dank years of absence.

I knew where to find the vials of Scorn. I slipped easily around poles and ancient machines. I felt like a shadow dancing unseen from corner to corner.

I stopped when I approached a locked door. I felt that there were people on the other side of it in the same way you can sense a presence over you when your eyes are closed. I could almost taste the metallic smell that assaulted my senses. I moved quickly, willing my dinner to stay in my stomach.

The container that held the Scorn was in the next room. I put my hand into it, thinking that I would take a handful of the vials and run, but my hand only grabbed air. I shoved my entire arm into the container, touching the bottom, but there were no vials of Scorn in it.

A man's laugh startled me. I whipped my hand out of the container and turned around to face him.

"They put it up on nights like tonight," he informed me.

"Where is it?" I asked before I could stop myself.

"Is that the reason you're really here?" he asked, advancing a step. "Did you really come here for another hand out?"

The man knew about the vial of Scorn I had been given during my last visit, but he wasn't the same man who had given it to me.

"Where is he?" I chanced, hoping he would tell me about the man with the limp.

The man stopped moving and cocked his head. "He thought you knew," he chuckled.

"Knew what?" I questioned automatically.

The man sighed audibly and threw up one of his hands. I made out the thin line of the shoulder strap he wore and the gun that was attached to it.

"He thought you figured it out, or she told you—" he started.

"Who's she?" I demanded.

"Look, kid," he said conversationally, advancing again, "I didn't sign up to give you a talk. That's up to the people who know you. We all thought you'd be here, but we assumed it'd be for different reasons. Anyway, you can't be here right now, so you need to leave."

I was baffled. *Where was the Scorn? Who should be telling me things? Who was "we"?*

The man wasn't going to hurt me, but I was unsure about the reason he showed restraint. His attitude was so casual that I was convinced that he knew way more about me than I knew about him.

A sound behind him refocused our attention. Aiden tried to back into the next room, but the man saw him before he could make it. The man raised his gun, and I instinctively darted between it and my friend.

"He's with me!" I shouted.

Bangs echoed in the next room as if they objected to the volume of my voice.

The man shushed me. "I can smell his father on him! Get out!" he hissed, pointing in the direction opposite to the one I had entered.

He may have meant for me to take the door, but I didn't want to risk getting trapped, so I grabbed Aiden's hand, and ran for the fallen beam. At first, it was hard for him to follow. His fear caused slower movements, but he picked up the pace when we reached the top of the beam.

He stooped through the window first and cursed. I bent my body to climb out, but a growl behind me caused me to fling my body out of the window and into the dumpster. I didn't stop once I lifted out of it. I ran to the other side of the street with my friend just behind me. I kept thinking that I would quit running when I felt safe, but every step I took felt like it was closely followed by whatever had growled at me. I finally felt protected under the streetlight just outside my subdivision.

Aiden and I grabbed our knees, heaving in gasps of cool air. It was several minutes before either of us could speak.

"What was that?" Aiden said. His husky voice hardly cut the night.

My breathing was a little more controlled. "I don't know. They must have guard dogs. I think someone was trying to scare us and keep us from going back there."

Aiden nodded. "I never want to go back there."

"You shouldn't have gone inside," I chastised. "I told you to stay outside and keep guard."

"I did," he said. "You didn't listen to me. I told you someone was going inside."

I traced a line along my lip with my thumb and sat on the pavement. I wanted to go home, but my legs were tingling. Aiden sat in front of me, presumably so that I could see in one direction and he could watch the other.

"Did you get it?" he asked.

I shook my head.

Aiden threw up his hands. "All of that and you didn't even get it?"

I glared at him. "It wasn't there."

"You said it was there."

"I know what I said," I barked at him. "The guy said it wasn't there tonight."

"Why not?"

"How should I know?" I yelled at him. "Do I look like a drug dealer?"

Our shouting had gotten the attention of a few dogs who yelped their displeasure.

"Actually, you're the one who suggested jumping out your window to go get drugs, so…"

I mumbled some expletives that would have made a sailor blush. Aiden laughed at me, and I pushed him. We stood face to face, breathing heavily. One movement by either one of us would have caused fists to fly.

Something changed after a moment. We didn't say anything, but Aiden backed away and dipped his head.

"You're bleeding," he remarked. "It's pretty bad."

I looked down at my dark shirt. I could smell more than see the blood. I felt a small stinging sensation in my midsection. When I lifted my shirt, a gash marked my stomach from my naval to my neck.

"It's when I jumped through the window," I told him.

We climbed the road to my house on shaky legs. I hoisted myself into the window and listened at the door. The rest of the house slept quietly while Aiden and I took turns washing off blood and dirt. I wadded up my ripped shirt, and I stuffed it into an empty cereal box I found in the trash can. I replaced it and hoped that my mom wouldn't see a bulge in the box before I carried out the trash the next morning.

Questions swirled around my mind when I cradled my pillow around my head. I wanted to consider the answers, but the adrenaline left my body as the sun's first rays filtered into my room.

CHAPTER TWENTY-ONE

Rowan stared at me with her hand on her hip. I tried to make my face unreadable.

"What does Mr. Sams say about traits?" she repeated.

"Some are dominant, and some are recessive," I answered vaguely.

"Which ones are dominant?" she pressed.

I rolled my eyes. "Widow's peak, brown eyes," I listed.

"Gold eyes, in your case," she commented.

I glanced away, self-conscious. Rowan was one of the most out-spoken girls in the class. She was witty and straight-forward, and I would have liked her if I wasn't convinced that she was somehow involved with the Scorn operation.

"Okay," she said loudly. "Ask me something."

Monique had paired us with study partners to quiz each other on the test material. I had glared my disapproval over her choice for me, but Monique ignored my stare.

"Can illnesses be passed from parent to offspring?" I read from my study guide on my desk. I had scribbled down the answer, but there was no way that Rowan would be able to read my almost illegible handwriting.

"Certain diseases can be passed, like some cancers and auto-immune disorders."

"What are some examples?" She was arrogant, and I wanted her to mess up. Maybe a hole in her knowledge would make her feel more real to me.

Rowan shrugged. "Leukemia and porphyria."

I almost jumped. My father was diagnosed with porphyria when he was young, and he had undergone several treatments for leukemia before he died. Leukemia was well-known, but porphyria was rare. The chances of Rowan putting both diseases together at once let me know that she had been digging into my past.

"I think you're ready for the test," I told her.

"There's no surprise there," Rowan remarked. "Does Mr. Sams give you the answers to the test?"

I narrowed my eyes. "No."

She clicked her pen several times. Finally, she shook her head and gave up on whatever answer she had expected.

"Time," Monique called.

The class moved sluggishly to their seats. Monique stood behind the most troublesome kids, herding them to their places.

I flew through the test. Monique had used a college prep, instead of the test she usually designed. It was a little harder than a basic multiple-choice test, but the answers were easy to locate.

I finished early, but I tried to pretend that I was still working. My eyes clipped to Monique, taking in her changed appearance.

There had been a substitute for three days. Monique had messaged my mom that she was having female issues, but I wasn't convinced. There were dark circles under her eyes when she came back to school, and she'd lost some weight. The skin under her eyes drooped, and there was almost a grayish hue to her skin. I was certain that she had used the Scorn she had taken from my room. I only hoped that it hadn't sent her over the edge.

◆

Rowan walked through the cafeteria line slowly, and stared at me, as if she expected me to invite her to my table. I tried to avoid her gaze by focusing on my food.

Loila noticed Rowan's stares and commented. "She can have my seat. I'm almost finished anyway."

There may have been a hint of jealousy in Loila's tone, but I didn't want to tease it out of her.

Aiden looked behind him.

"Hey," I called. "Could you be less obvious?"

"What?" he said. "She's eye candy."

I was thankful when he turned around. Tabitha grabbed her purse suddenly and fished out a tube of lip balm. She didn't need it in the middle of her meal, so it was a clear sign that she was nervous about Aiden's interest in Rowan.

"Hey, Razz," Rowan said to the back of my head when she passed. I didn't move. When I didn't give her the reaction she wanted, she added, "Hey, Aiden."

"Hello," he spoke deeply. Rowan giggled, and Loila raised her eyebrows and huffed. Tabitha stared at the food on her plastic fork.

"How do you guys think you did on the test?" Rowan asked.

We all grumbled noncommittedly.

"I think Razz and I did the best," she bragged. "He finishes around the same time as me, and he doesn't think anyone notices when he waits to turn in his work." She put her hand on my shoulder.

"You wait to turn in your test?" Aiden asked.

"He just doesn't want to be the first person to turn it in," Loila said dismissively. She was trying hard not to look at Rowan's hand on my shoulder.

Rowan mocked her with a laugh. "Oh, Lila, you're so quaint."

Loila didn't correct Rowan when she misspoke her name. The girls stared at each other.

"I'm going to get another milk," I declared, removing Rowan's hand, and excusing myself from the awkward situation.

Rowan had seated herself where she could watch me. I avoided her steady gaze.

Loila left the lunchroom as soon as the bell rang. She bolted out the door so fast that Tabitha couldn't match her pace.

"I'm going to ask Rowan to the banquet," Aiden announced. I didn't protest, so my friend approached Rowan. He sat down, said something that made him laugh, and waited for her response.

I didn't ask him about the outcome, but I could tell it was bothering him. He waited until we were in a throng of seventh and eighth graders before he revealed her answer to me.

"She said that she was waiting on someone else to ask her," he informed me. "I think she means you."

"Then she'll be waiting forever."

"I'm going to ask someone else."

"How about Tabitha?" I suggested.

Aiden scrunched up his face. "She's cute, but my dad wouldn't like her. She's adopted."

"I wouldn't worry about what he had to say about it," I said and immediately regretted it. I could almost feel Aiden's guard go up. He didn't speak to me again until after our math class.

We worked our way through angles on graphs, and we met Loila on our way to our fourth class. Her face was flushed, and tears threatened to spill over. "I forgot to do my English homework."

"Wow! Even I read my short story," Aiden said.

"Don't rub it in," Loila choked out. She was nearing a break down.

"I read 'The Tell-Tale Heart', but you can discuss it," I offered.

"I don't know what it's about," Loila said, but the storm was clearing from her eyes.

I pulled my notes from my pocket and unfolded the paper. A photocopied picture of Edgar Allan Poe slipped out, and we all strained to catch it before it hit the floor. I grabbed it between two fingers and handed it to Loila. "You can read my notes, and you should be able to get a good idea about it."

Loila accepted the notes gratefully, but then she stopped. "What about you?"

"I read 'A Rose for Emily' last year, and I can bring up some good points about it," I assured her.

"Is that the one where she feeds her husband to the cops?" Aiden asked.

I chuckled. "No. I think you have it confused with another story."

"Or maybe a Stephen King novel," Loila laughed.

CHAPTER TWENTY-TWO

"You could polish it faster," my mom told Lexi. Lexi bent over our grandmother's silver and rubbed the piece in her hand more vigorously.

I glanced up from my phone, suddenly aware that my mom was upset. She rushed around the room, stuffing papers in drawers and straightening pictures.

"Can I help?"

"I don't know, Razzberry," she answered. "If you see something that needs to be done then do it."

It was uncommon for my mom to allow herself to get so frazzled, but she had planned a special dinner. Monique had been given a highly coveted, tenure position at Pale Woods Academy. Monique didn't make a big deal out of it, but my mom fussed that she needed a celebration. When Monique balked at the suggestion of a party, my mom compromised with a dinner in honor of her accomplishment.

My mom, Lexi, and I had dressed up, but Monique arrived in a college tee shirt and a pair of jeans. She had dabbed on a little makeup and put new purple streaks in her hair, though. Vanilla fragrance puffed off her when she stepped through the door, hardly masking the aroma of the felines she had allowed to lounge on her clothes.

"Why did I have to wear this itchy dress?" Lexi complained. "Monique didn't wear a dress!"

"She's right, Allison," Monique said to our mom. "She can change if she wants to."

"No one is changing," my mom asserted. "You wouldn't let me give you a proper celebration—"

"Tenure is hardly a reason for you to throw a party," Monique said flatly. She was embarrassed by all the attention.

"Everyone else who gets tenure has a party," my mom countered. "Anita Hughes had cake and ice cream in the teacher's lounge last year when she got tenure. Years ago, Grigori turned this place inside out to celebrate when I —." She stopped when the memory hit her. Lexi held onto every word and waited expectantly for more. The details were valuable to her since she didn't have memories of our father. My mom shook the recollection from her mind. "Now let's have a wonderful meal."

Monique shuffled to our kitchen, gently pushing party balloons out of her way. The aroma from the celebratory dinner delivered scents from various sources. The most prominent of the smells was from the cabbage steaks and the multilayer cake.

"I said I liked *steak*," Monique smirked to herself when she saw the cabbage steaks. She stifled a laugh.

"They're still steaks," my mom defended.

"The person who said this is a steak is missing their tastebuds," Monique remarked, gesturing to the vegetables covered in olive oil and spices. "But I appreciate the gesture." My mom smiled at her friend, and we took our places at the table.

My mom had placed a magenta table runner with rearing gold lions across the middle of our oak dining table. I had polished the wood while my sister had cleaned our grandmother's silver. All the surfaces had been scrubbed to perfection, thankfully, without our mom's help. She had exhausted herself by preparing the food, and we didn't want her to completely drain herself by trying to clean.

Monique was the guest of honor, so I pulled out a chair at the head of the table for her. She stopped and stared at me, amused and bothered by my gesture. After she noticed my mom looking at us, Monique rolled her eyes and sat in the chair.

Monique's color was a little better, but her skin still possessed a gray hue. She ate heartily, and I hoped my mom's vegetable dinner would give her the nutrients she needed to bounce back.

"You will never believe what Emma did today," Lexi started, beginning our usual round of polite dinnertime chatter.

My mom put her finger up. She was chewing food, but when she finished, she reminded her, "This is Monique's special dinner. No drama tonight."

After our mom lowered her eyes to cut another bite of food, Lexi shook her head and flicked peas around her plate with her fork. "So, how was your day at work, Monique?" she monotoned.

"I had a good day," Monique answered. "Now tell me what Emma did."

"My mom opened her mouth to interject, but Monique raised her hand. "I am truly interested in the trials of a second grader."

Lexi perked up, ignoring our mom's piercing stare, and launched into her tale. "Emma is dating this boy named Jason."

"*Dating*?" my mom interrupted. She only believed a couple was dating if they went on actual dates.

"It's what it's *called*, Mom," Lexi sighed. After our mom busied herself with salting her food, my sister continued. "Anyway, Jason asked her to play this puzzle with him a million times. It has the states and capitals on it, but I think he really likes the colors. The teacher said something about him being color blind once, because he really liked the greens and reds of the puzzle, and—"

"What did Emma do?" my mom asked Lexi, seeing the divergence from the topic and quickly steering my sister back to her point.

"So, Emma was completely fed up with playing the puzzle," Lexi went on. "but she didn't want to hurt Jason's feelings. So, she got to school early this morning and hid the puzzle."

My sister smiled widely, as if we should understand the punchline of a joke before she delivered it. "Jason was looking for it everywhere! Emma just sat there like she didn't know where it was!"

Lexi continued to laugh at her own story. Monique and I smiled at her mirth, but my mom was disappointed.

"That poor boy," she said, aghast. "That puzzle made him happy, and Emma took it away from him. Isn't she supposed to like him?" Her question was meant to make Lexi feel guilty about repeating the boy's misfortune. She didn't expect an answer. "If it's the same Jason I remember, he was in my class last year. He was a very nice boy."

"He *is* nice, but—" my sister interjected.

"No," my mom said. "There's no reason that the puzzle should have been hidden." She pointed at my sister. "In fact, you should have pretended that you found the puzzle while everyone helped him search for it."

"No one helped him look for it."

My mom took a deep breath, glowering at my sister. "Why didn't the class help him search for it?" She spoke each word through gritted teeth.

"Because it's *annoying*," Lexi whined. "We all knew that she put it in her locker, but we were glad he couldn't find it."

My mother's cheeks burned a pretty shell pink that made her look like a porcelain doll, painted with too much blush. "I am *so* disappointed in you. First of all, you will get the puzzle out of Emma's locker and give it to Jason. Next, you will apologize to him, and thirdly, you will tell him that you watched Emma hide it."

Lexi's eyes grew wide. "But, Mom, all the kids will *hate* me!"

"People deserve to know the truth." My mom's voice cracked, and a tear spilled out of her eye. "They need to know if the person they love isn't who they say they are!"

The conversation had taken a turn from Emma and Jason to my mom and my dad. Monique sensed it and struggled to change the subject.

"Hey, Razz," she said jovially. "You haven't eaten anything."

I decided to try the cabbage steaks. I picked up my fork and pushed around the layers until I had a reasonable bite.

My mom bolted from the table, upset by her conversation with my sister and frustrated that Monique's celebratory dinner had been tainted. I shrugged at Monique and tasted the vegetable my mom had made to replace the flank of a steer.

As soon as I took the bite, it felt like I had been electrocuted. I spit the cabbage out immediately, but my reaction continued. My throat threatened to close, my nose burned, and my eyes watered. I was vaguely aware that Monique had sprung up from her chair so fast that it had tumbled over. My body slid onto the ground and shook. The best I could do was to make the universal choking sign, even though having my hands close to my neck made me want to rip out my own throat.

I vomited onto the floor. It was mostly water, tinged in red with bits of food. I didn't think my throat would allow anything to pass, but I watched the result pool around me as my stomach emptied.

Monique dipped into her pocket and pulled out a vial. She rubbed a foul-tasting liquid across my tongue.

Lexi screamed for our mom. Fear had frozen her to her chair until Monique had rushed to my rescue.

My mom ran to my side, flung me onto my back, and tried to figure out the best approach to help me.

"He's going to be okay now," Monique told her.

I was gasping for air, but it started to feel like my lungs were finally filling with precious oxygen. The burning had lessened from an all-consuming fire to an uncomfortable sunburn.

I was able to sit up, and I noticed that my mom's knee was in my vomit. Monique's clothes were covered in the stringy remains of my last meal. The whole room smelled like blood and burned hair.

"I called them, Mommy," my sister said. She reserved the use of the endearment when she was truly scared.

"Thank you, Lexi," our mom spoke. "Razzberry, the ambulance will be here soon. I'm going to ride with you."

"He's going to be okay," Monique repeated. She seemed to be pushing the point on my mom, but my mom was unaffected by it. She stared back at Monique.

"Don't you care?" she asked, disgusted. "My son almost died, and you don't want him to go to the hospital?"

"I just meant that he's okay," Monique sighed. "He's up, and he seems to be fine, so whatever happened has passed."

"But what caused it?" my mom pressed. "Why does my son look pale and scared?"

I tried to speak, but my tongue felt a little too large for my mouth. My mom abandoned her argument with Monique to comfort me.

"It's okay," she soothed. "We'll find out what happened, so you won't have to go through that again."

I couldn't be certain, but I thought I saw Monique roll her eyes.

CHAPTER TWENTY-THREE

I waited in the emergency room for four hours before I saw a doctor. The ambulance ride had been short, and Monique drove closely behind with Lexi, who had used the situation to her advantage by extorting a ride in the passenger seat. My mode of arrival had nothing to do with the severity of my condition, so I was placed in the hallway until more serious cases were assessed.

I asked my mom if we could leave several times, but she asserted that we needed to find out the cause of my sudden reaction. Monique remained silent, except to entertain Lexi. Finally, she gave up on repetitive games of I Spy, and handed my sister her phone to watch videos.

After our prolonged wait, a nurse unceremoniously escorted us to a room that was about the size of walk-in closet. My family squeezed in behind me, and Monique sat in the only chair with Lexi on her lap. The nurse took my blood pressure and temperature, and she started an IV of cold saline.

The nurse asked for the specifics of my condition and an estimate of my pain. I offered her the best version of the incident that led to my arrival and rated my pain at a four.

"Why are you at a four?" my mom asked, concerned that I had categorized my pain at a more than tolerable level to convenience the nurse.

"It's been painful to be here for four hours," I replied, earning a stern look from the nurse and a smirk from Monique. My mom shook her head, embarrassed.

The doctor breezed into the room, flipping the papers on my chart. He shook my hand and introduced himself to my family.

"Rasputin," he remarked. "Are you a history buff?" he asked my mom.

"His father was," she replied.

The past tense of the verb she used put the doctor's focus back on my condition. Death makes most people uncomfortable, even if they deal with the possibility of seeing it every day. "So, you ate something that caused a reaction?"

"He had a cabbage steak, with olive oil, garlic, and black pepper," my mom volunteered.

"Have you had them before and had a reaction?" the doctor asked, continuing to address me.

I shook my head. "I haven't had cabbage steak before, but my mom puts cabbage in her spring rolls."

The doctor nodded. "Your temperature and blood pressure are elevated, so you could have contracted a virus. We'll draw some blood to rule out a bacterial infection."

Monique sighed, but the doctor ignored her. He grabbed my hand and studied it.

"How long have you had this discoloration?"

I stared at my hand, surprised to see a grayish hue on top of it. "I don't know," I answered honestly.

"What kinds of vitamins does he take?" the doctor asked my mom.

"It's just a regular multi-vitamin," she responded, straining to understand the logic in his questioning.

"I think I may have found the reason for your son's condition."

Monique jerked to attention. Lexi wabbled on her legs, still more interested in the game on Monique's phone than the unfolding conversation.

"I think your son has argyria." When we all appeared baffled, he clarified, "He has ingested colloidal silver."

Monique paled. She busied herself with helping my sister load another game.

The doctor turned to me. "Have you taken anything you weren't supposed to take, like recreational drugs or something from the lab at school?"

"What?" my mom said. "He's a good boy. He has never sampled drugs."

I saw the doctor's skepticism, but he didn't reveal his feelings to my mom.

"I'm his science teacher," Monique piped up. "There's nothing missing from my lab."

The doctor nodded, more satisfied with Monique's affirmation than my mom's biased statement. "You may want to check his multivitamin," he warned. "Something has left a deposit on his skin, and you need to locate the source so that it doesn't damage his internal organs."

"He could have damaged his organs?" my mom cried.

"It's possible," the doctor replied. "We can run the tests here, and you can pay the emergency room costs, or we can call it an isolated reaction, and you can take him to your primary care physician."

"Do you really think it's argyria?" my mom asked.

"The symptoms you reported, coupled with the gray area on his hand" — he stated, lifting my hand as evidence — "certainly suggest it." He noticed my mom's defeated posture and softened his approach. "Rasputin should be fine. Just make him an appointment with his primary care doctor as soon as possible."

"Will this ever go away?" I asked, flashing the small area of silver on my hand.

"No," the doctor answered resolutely. "You can have your skin lasered to remove it, though."

My mom visibly relaxed. I tensed at the thought of laser surgery. My mom considered laser removal a viable option, but my family's finances would never allow the aesthetic treatment.

Twenty minutes later, we loaded into Monique's car. My sister kept glaring at me from her side of the car.

"We were there *forever!*" she complained.

"We know a little more about what's going on with your brother," our mom said.

Lexi crossed her arms and stared out the window. Her warm breath made tiny clouds on her cold reflection.

"I guess we can start calling you Silver Hand," Monique teased. The joke fell flat, and she made no more attempts to lift the emotional temperature in the car.

Monique tried to help us clean up, but my mom made her go home as soon as she dropped us off at our house. I wasn't excited about the sight and smell of vomit that had spent hours soaking into our floors, but I hoped we could clean it quickly.

"Hey, Razz," Monique called to me while my mom was unlocking the entrance.

I dipped my head level with her open passenger side window. She appeared to be having an inner struggle. It was clear that she wanted to tell me something, but she couldn't find the right words. Finally, she gave up and said, "See ya later, Silver Hand."

I tilted my grin and forced a chuckle, patting the car hood twice and backing up so she could leave. Something nagged at me about Monique, but I didn't know what bothered me about my mom's long-time friend and my future guardian.

CHAPTER TWENTY-FOUR

Whispers dotted the hallways. I had fine-tuned my attention to miss the drama that circulated, but the news was so big that it found my apathetic ears.

"She cussed her out," Aiden told me proudly, stuffing the rest of a banana into his mouth.

We walked into our first period class, and the uproar was palpable. Students were gathered in groups, exchanging different perspectives of the same event.

"Is she suspended?" I asked my friend.

"No. Mrs. Holt didn't even give her detention! She just let it go."

"She's pretty strict," I commented. "Do you really think it's over?"

"Yeah," he confirmed. "I saw it, and Mrs. Holt didn't even go to the office after Rowan finished yelling at her. She just walked back into her classroom."

Mr. Fritz calmed everyone with a stern look. His scraping chalk announced the beginning of class, and the students shuffled to their seats.

He passed out our graded tests, stopping at Loila's desk and tapping her paper. "I'll need to speak to you after class."

Loila was embarrassed, but she didn't seem surprised. Loila usually made good grades, so I wondered about the reason Mr. Fritz wanted to see her. I stayed just outside the door after the bell rang and waited on her. She startled when she noticed me.

"Were you waiting to talk to Mr. Fritz?" she asked.

"I was waiting to talk to you," I replied.

"Why?"

Loila wasn't going to be forthright with me without prodding, so I said, "How did you do on the test?"

"It was fine."

"Okay," I said, realizing that Loila didn't want me to pursue the subject. I tried another avenue. "How's cheerleading?"

That subject didn't improve her mood. She pursed her lips and tightened her hands around her laptop. "Fine." As I rebounded from her curt reply, she added, "They're having a sleepover at my house after the banquet."

She had provided me with a way in to ask her to the banquet. Instead, I fumbled, "*They* are having a sleepover? Wouldn't *you* be having a sleepover if it's at your house?

"Yeah, sure."

"It could be fun," I prompted.

Loila nodded and stared down the hall. It wasn't the first time I felt like all the happiness had been drained from her.

"Loila," I said confidentially. I hardly ever used a humorless tone, so she quickly gave me her full attention. "I think you should quit the cheerleading squad."

"I can't," she sighed. "I made a commitment."

"You've already asked them, haven't you?" I realized, referring to her parents. Her silence clarified the situation for me. "They won't let you quit, so you're trying to fail. Then the school will kick you off the squad because of your grades."

Her face reddened in a flash. "I'm not trying to *fail*. I'm just trying to get my grades low enough before midterms, but then I can bring them back up before the end of the year."

She had revealed her plan to me, and I didn't want to lose her trust. Her confession made me more nervous, though. I decided to push her a little more.

"It must be pretty bad," I fished.

Loila shrugged. "Practices aren't hard. We do drills that I can do in my sleep."

I waited for her to go on. We were getting close to Monique's classroom, and I worried that my window of opportunity would close when second period started. I had to press a little harder.

"I meant the Rituals. They can be pretty brutal."

"What do you know about the Rituals?" Loila snapped. The window of opportunity slammed shut on my fingers. "My dad doesn't believe they happen, and my mom thinks it's just like a cute game of Truth or Dare. Well, it's not the same as it was when she was a cheerleader!" Several heads turned in our direction, and Loila closed her mouth with a snap.

"What *is* it like?" I chanced.

"Stop it," Loila whispered. "No one gets it." She slouched into Monique's room, ducking our teacher's exposing stare.

As I passed, Monique raised her eyebrows to communicate her concern. I shrugged almost imperceptibly and took my seat.

Monique had recovered from her illness, or drug hangover, and she taught forcefully. She only had a month left to impart the knowledge and skills all eighth graders should know. Her sense of urgency was contagious, and most of the class scribbled vigorously while she spoke.

I noticed Loila's head dip every few moments. She wasn't busy writing notes during the lecture, and she looked down every time Monique turned around. I wondered what she was writing, and to whom she was texting. All her close friends, and most of the cheerleaders were in our class.

"Loila, can you tell us about the reason for the reaction?" Monique asked. She turned around and crossed her arms.

Loila stared back at her with wide eyes. Her arm moved slightly, covering her phone under her sleeve.

"Really?" Monique persisted. "No answer? I'm not surprised. But who can pay attention in class when they have another pressing matter?"

Loila was frozen. Her frustration and fear hit me in an almost tangible way. I tasted her emotions and shook my head to clear it.

Monique held out her hand. Loila stared back at her, afraid to move, hopeful that she could retain her phone. Monique flicked her fingers into her palm, creating a swift scratching sound, a strong indication that she expected Loila to comply immediately.

Loila rose from her seat and handed Monique her phone. She disgracefully returned to her desk.

"You can have it back at the end of the day," Monique told her.

Loila jumped. "The end of the day!" she shouted.

Monique held her composure. "Yes, Loila," she spoke evenly. "The handbook says that I have to turn it in to the principal, but it's your first offense, so you can have it back at the end of the day." Loila's face betrayed her resentment. "Is there something you'd like to add?"

Loila shook her head, but she sat back and crossed her arms. She watched Monique slide out her bottom drawer and toss her phone inside it. In defiance, she didn't take notes with the rest of the class when our teacher resumed the lecture.

I ran to catch up with Loila at the end of class. I thought she was going to yell at me, but she asked, "Your mom's friends with her. Can you ask her to give me back my phone?"

I thought the reason Loila's phone was sitting in the desk drawer instead of the office was because my mom was friends with Monique and I was friends with Loila, but I didn't express my feeling to Loila. Instead, I shook my head. "It might make it worse."

"Aaah!" Loila yelled into the air, startling a sixth grader. She didn't notice his distress. "Can you just ask her?' she begged me.

"If I ask her for your phone, she's probably going to keep it," I admitted honestly.

"Why?"

"Because she's going to think that I was the one sending you messages during class."

"Oh," Loila realized.

I matched her pace, and smells of barbequed pork wafted down the hall to greet us.

"You weren't texting me, were you?" I teased.

"No," Loila replied with enough snarkiness to cause me to recoil, and she backpedaled. "I'm sorry, Razz. It was an important conversation, but now I doubt that the other person will talk to me in the same way again."

Loila was completely deflated. At lunch, Aiden tried to joke with her about the incident, but she didn't perk up. She dipped a fry in her ketchup and swirled it around, but she didn't eat it.

Monique filled a tray and sat down with the other eighth grade teachers. The principal liked for the students to see the teachers eating to make them seem like everyday people. Instead of making teachers more approachable, it distanced us further. The teachers interacted with one another like there was an invisible barrier between them and the students who shared the same lunchroom.

Moisture pooled in Loila's eyes. She tried to turn away before a tear rolled down her nose.

Finally, I had seen enough. Whatever was important to Loila was on the phone, and I wanted to help her.

"You may not be able to get your phone back until the end of the day, but I can buy you some time to read your messages and respond to them," I told her.

Aiden stopped in mid-sentence, unaware that his story had been largely ignored. Tabitha winced, but she kept her misgivings to herself.

"How?" Loila asked.

I revealed each part of my plan to my friends. I tried not to steal glances at Monique as I spoke, but my traitorous eyes pulled to her several times. If she noticed my stare, she didn't acknowledge it. Most likely, she would have assumed that our table was discussing our displeasure over the action she took against Loila. We left the cafeteria in our usual way, careful not to deviate from our pattern.

Tabitha lingered just outside of the cafeteria, phone in hand. "I'll let you know as soon as Mr. Sams leaves," she promised.

Aiden, Loila, and I almost ran down the hallway. Aiden stayed outside the door, gripping the doorframe. His usually careless demeanor was replaced with beaded perspiration and concern. "You'll know she's here if you hear me talking," he said. "I don't know why you need your phone so bad," he addressed Loila and started to ramble. "My dad will kill me if I get another detention."

"If you get another detention, you'll be suspended," Loila reminded him.

"Exactly," he returned.

The locks on the classroom doors were a joke. They were a basic pin tumbler lock that you could find on the front doors of most of the houses in our tiny town. I pulled out my lock pick set from my wallet, surprising my friends.

"You carry that around all the time?" Loila asked.

"Yeah," I answered absentmindedly and started working.

Aiden's shadow fell over me. "Is that even legal?"

"You can buy the kits anywhere," Loila informed him. "I think it's only illegal in Nevada and Ohio to carry it."

"And Virginia," I added. "The state has a law that says that you can get in trouble just for having it."

"Why?" Aiden said.

"Because if you have a lock pick set in those states then they believe you mean to use them to commit a crime," Loila responded.

"How do *you* know about it?" Aiden asked Loila.

"I'm smart," Loila replied in disgust, motioning to the walls of our accelerated academy. "And I used to read spy novels," she added.

"I go to school here, too, and I didn't know it," Aiden mumbled.

Aiden attended Pale Woods Academy because his father had a lot of money. He made decent grades, but he struggled to keep up with the academic content in his classes. He could have done better if he applied himself, but he was too busy playing video games to study.

My lock picking kit had been a gift from my dad, but I didn't want to talk to my friends about the times he and I had used it before his death. Instead, I concentrated on my task. I inserted the tension wrench quickly, relying on my friends to watch for teachers and student informants. I lifted pins with my pick until they were all past the shear line. I scrubbed my pick back and forth. I lifted up when I pulled the pin back until all the pins were set. A click announced my success.

"That was fast," Aiden commented. "How many times have you done that?"

"A few," I admitted.

Loila slipped inside when I opened the door and bounced in place. I could almost hear her teeth chatter as her adrenaline spiked.

I opened the desk drawer and produced her phone quickly. After I handed it to her, she scanned her messages, turning pale. I gave her privacy by turning my attention to the rest of the contents in Monique's drawer.

I found bobble heads that nodded their agreement with my deception, unopened notes between friends and puppy-eyed couples, sealed drinks, and bags of chips. It was a treasure trove of adolescent contraband, and I wanted more to show for my experience than my friends' knowledge. I grabbed a bag of plain potato chips for us to share, and I spied something that caused the blood in my body to turn cold.

Aiden said something, but I was too consumed by my find to understand his words or what they meant. Loila shoved her phone in my face and broke me from my reverie. I tossed her phone back into the drawer and slammed it.

"She's coming," she mouthed at me.

We were trapped. We couldn't climb out the windows, and it was too late to go through the door. Aiden's words were coming out like machine fire, in an attempt to stall our teacher. I formed a plan quickly and put it into action.

"What is going on here?" Monique demanded.

I broke away from Loila's lips and faked a stunned response. "I-I thought you were still at lunch."

"What are you doing in my classroom?" Monique barked. "I locked the door before I left."

"I picked the lock," I told her truthfully.

Monique measured me. I tried to elicit the suave demeanor of a young man who was used to the attentions of a beautiful girl. I failed.

"Did you get your phone?" Monique asked Loila.

"I don't have it," she replied honestly. She looked away from everyone, but she didn't release her loose hold on my arms. The situation was most embarrassing for her. The students who learned about our kiss would slip me high-fives, and the teachers might wink sly eyes at me, but an unspoken double-standard caused Loila to feel shame over our kiss. We weren't in a relationship, so her actions could be viewed as a lack of self-confidence leading to a swirling decline of her reputation instead of a natural biological response. Our kiss had really been a complete sham that we had traded against getting caught pilfering through Monique's desk drawer. We hoped the punishment would be lighter.

"Well, I guess I know who you were texting now," Monique remarked, looking pointedly at me.

"Can Loila have her phone back?" I tried. "I promise that I won't message her for the rest of the day."

Monique sighed heavily. "Yeah, sure." She moved us aside and pulled the phone off the pile she had collected. "Loila had to be desperate to get her phone back since she was willing to pretend that she was in here making out with you."

"Hey!"

Aiden and Loila laughed. "It wasn't all that bad, Mr. Sams," she joked. They joined in more laughter while my ego shattered on the floor.

Tabitha was waiting for us in the hallway. We joined her and waited until we were lost in the commotion of moving bodies before we spoke.

"You were supposed to text us!" Loila reprimanded her.

"I did," Tabitha stressed. "But then I thought that you might not have your phone yet, and I was going to text Razz, but Mr. Sams saw me. She started talking to me, and she told me to walk with her."

I was the only one who understood that Monique had suspected us as soon as we had left the lunchroom. "What did she talk to you about?"

"She asked me who I was going to the banquet with," Tabitha said, looking down at her feet. Loila and I both glanced at Aiden, but he was too daft to pick up on the pointed silence.

"She knew where we were when she saw you by yourself," I told Tabitha, seeing the flaw in my plan.

"At least you got to kiss Loila," Aiden said cheerfully, winking at me. He held up his hand and moved his eyes from me to it, indicating that he wanted a high five. I ignored my friend's invitation, but he didn't drop his extra-wide smile.

"You kissed Razz?" Tabitha blurted out before she slapped a hand over her mouth.

Loila cocked her head like she was trying to consider the best answer. "It was nice. He surprised me." Her beautiful dimples winked at me.

My heart skipped several beats and I briefly forgot how to form words. I could feel so much heat on my face that I started to sweat, and I opened my mouth without thinking. "I had to kiss her. I didn't want Monique to think we broke into her classroom for Loila's phone."

It was the truth, but it hurt Loila. She had given me a compliment, and I had ruined it by acting like I had done it to save myself from the repercussions of our deviance. I could almost feel the temperature drop between Loila and me.

No one spoke again until we were in our third period class. Rowan spied me and sat down in the seat in front of me. She turned around as if she had just noticed me.

"I want to go to the banquet," she declared.

I raised my eyebrows. "Okay. Go then."

"Silly boy," she laughed with no sincerity. "I want you to take me to the banquet."

"I'm not going."

Rowan feigned hurt. "I thought we were friends, Razz. I just wanted to go to the banquet with someone nice."

A couple of people near us moved their heads, and I wondered why she wanted me to take her to the banquet. *Was it because no one else in the school liked her?* Well, almost no one.

"Aiden would take you," I offered. "He's nice."

As if on cue, Aiden slid to one knee in front of Rowan. "Lady Rowan," he addressed her formally. "Will you grace me with your presence at the banquet?"

Rowan's face folded in an unusual way. It was a look of disgust, embarrassment, and acceptance at the same time.

"Sure," she responded curtly and turned in her seat to face the front of the room.

Aiden wasn't fazed. He fist-bumped a couple of the other boys in the class before he settled down in one of the seats in the back row. He made loud kissing noises until our teacher silenced him. Rowan took his immaturity in stride, but she must have been wondering about what I considered "nice."

An insistent sleet pelted the window, as if it were waging its last battle against the recent spring warmth. For the first time since Monique caught me in her room, I was able to slow my thoughts. I wanted to concentrate on math class, but my mind kept going back to what I had seen in Monique's drawer.

I had acted fast when Loila had handed me her phone. I had popped it into the drawer and had asked her if I could kiss her within seconds. Loila didn't see what I found among Monique's treasures or my reaction to it. In her panic, she was too busy to notice what I slipped into my pocket.

CHAPTER TWENTY-FIVE

"Why did you break into Monique's desk?" my mom asked me.

"I didn't break into her desk."

"Rasputin Grigori, cut the crap!"

My mom only used my first and middle names if I was in a lot of trouble. I understood the severity of the situation, but I adopted an air of casual indifference in hopes that my mom would find humor in it.

"I didn't break into her *desk*," I clarified. "I broke into her *room*." It was a childish distinction, but I was proud of myself, until my mom threw up her skeletal hands. I didn't want her to become too agitated in her fragile state, so I added, "I did it for Loila."

My mom crossed the room and slung a pot of warm water on the stove. "Yeah. Monique told me you were in her room to make out, but Loila couldn't care less about you."

"She said the kiss was nice," I reported.

My mom spun to face me, pointing her finger. "Ha! You and Loila weren't there to make out. You just admitted that it was *one* kiss."

"I didn't have enough time for another one," I joked.

My mom grabbed a pan, abusing the stove eyes again as she put it down too hard. "Why did you do that to poor Monique?" she demanded. "How am I supposed to ask her to keep you and your sister when I"— she collected herself and continued—"when I'm gone if you are going to use her feelings for you as leverage for you and your friends to get what you want."

"I'm not going to use Monique," I promised. "You're right, Mom. It was a dumb idea."

"So, you'll apologize to her?"

"Yeah, I'll talk to her tomorrow before class."

Now that my mom was pacified, I felt like I was in a good position to talk to her. She had already been upset, so I wouldn't ruin a potentially good mood.

"Can you tell me what you remember about Dad," I asked.

My mom stopped peeling potatoes. Even though her back was turned to me, I could feel her closing me out. "There's nothing to talk about," she shrugged. "He had a family, and he abandoned us for bigger and better things."

"But what if he didn't," I suggested.

"Enough!" my mom yelled. The water bubbled on the stove while my mom took a few deep breaths. "I understand that you want to know about the man who sired you, but I don't have anything nice to say anymore. Any beautiful memory we had together has been tainted by his absence."

"I used to go see him," I confided.

"You what?" She grabbed the counter for support. Her head hung between her shoulder blades.

I had dipped my toe into a pool of my mom's emotions, found it cold, and decided to cannonball into the water. "I used to hang out in old houses with him," I went on. "He was hiding from someone."

"Then why was he giving so many interviews," my mom scoffed.

"I don't know," I admitted. "Maybe he was trying to make it harder for someone to kill him."

"It just doesn't make sense," my mom argued. "He left. He left all of us, even if you snuck around and saw him. I'm sure it was on his own terms."

"I was there when the bear attacked him."

My mom spun on me. "What did you say?" Her outrage turned to sadness and then acceptance. "It makes sense."

"He used to meet me after school. We would walk to old houses and—"

"You broke into them," she finished for me.

"Yeah," I admitted. "I knew we shouldn't do it, but we didn't take anything, and Dad said the person who owned the houses had taken something from him."

My mom nodded, folding her arms into her frail frame. I had thought of her as other-worldly, a figure whose strength was unmatched, but her skin sagged on her petite form, and her full lips stayed dry and chapped. I considered what my words were doing to her and then I thought about my guilt if I missed my chance to confess.

She held out her hand. I took it and put my other one over it. She sat down in the chair beside me and listened attentively to my account. "He camped at the river," I said. "He had a little boat, a kayak or something, that he said would help him get away if they came after him."

"Did he tell you who 'they' are?" my mom asked gently.

"No," I admitted. "But I didn't ask him. I thought he meant the police would come get him because we broke into all of those houses."

"What was he looking for in the houses?"

"He said it was a notebook or paper he wrote," I recalled. "He said that he had found the Fountain of Youth, and they had stolen it from him."

"He was always obsessed with his experiments," my mom remembered. "He spent hours at his facility, trying to prove his newest idea. I hated when he started taking drugs. He had a beautiful mind."

"How did you know he took drugs?"

"I saw the needle marks on his arm," she said, letting out a long breath. "And let's face it, he was delusional. He talked about seeing monsters."

I wasn't going to confirm or deny my father's sanity, and my mom sensed it. She urged me to go on with a half-smile and a tap on my hand.

"I was in the tent when I heard something growling," I recounted. "He usually camped near the river, but he had hiked to a spot near an old town."

"Lost Cove," my mom guessed.

"I think that's what he called it. We went to the town, or what was left of it, before it was dark, and he fried some squirrel for us and we hung out by the campfire afterward."

"Where was I?" my mom inquired sternly. "I don't remember allowing you to freely roam the night at eight years old."

"I told you that I was spending the night with Aiden," I admitted.

"You did that a lot back then," she responded knowingly. "Was it so that you could sneak away and spend time with your father?"

"Not every time," I said, lowering my head to hide the shame I felt for lying to my mom. "But most of the time."

She nodded her understanding. "I was strict. I didn't let you see him because he was unbalanced, and he didn't have a place to stay."

I didn't want to argue my best interests as a child and the love I had for my father. Due to his mental illness, my mom's father had been unfair to her mother. My mom had felt the effects of her father's abuse, so when my father fell into similar patterns, she thought she was protecting me from an unstable parent.

"When we were looking around the buildings in Lost Cove, I found a broken vial," I continued. "Dad got it from me and put it into his coat pocket. After we ate the squirrel, he asked me to go get it out of his coat. I found the coat, but I couldn't find the vial. That's when I heard growling.

"Dad told me to stay in the tent," I recounted. "He yelled at the bear, but I couldn't move." My voice broke, and my mom squeezed my hands. After I trusted myself to talk, I said, "I heard them thrashing around, grunting and huffing. I think he burned the bear at some point, but the burn only made it madder."

My mind drifted off as I told the story, and I could see the shadows the firelight threw up against the tent walls. I wanted to help my father battle the bear, but I could only hold his jacket in my useless hands. I don't know how long I stayed in the tent before I felt it was safe enough to peek out.

"I called for him, Mom, but he was gone."

"It's okay, Razzberry," she consoled, wrapping me in an extended hug.

"They didn't find his body for days, but I knew he was gone," I wailed. I didn't know when I had started crying, but my tears were dripping off my face and onto my mom's understanding shoulders. Her bones protruded from her skin, and I feared hurting her, so I pulled away long before I was ready.

"I was going to go to Aiden's house to tell you that they were looking for your father, but you were already home when I stopped to pick up Lexi from our neighbor," she surmised. "I thought you had heard about it from someone else and had come home early."

I remembered that my mom had found me crying in the shower. "I paid a hiker to report my father's fight with the bear," I told her.

I had searched for my father, following a trail of blood that had ended abruptly. When he didn't answer my whispered calls, I ran hard and fast down the trails. I was so terrified that I almost didn't see the group of young hikers before I stumbled into their campsite.

They tried to get me to stay with them, but I told them that I was a runaway from a bad foster care situation, so they left me out of their report. My lie gave me just enough time to get home and shower before my mom got there.

"You were a very brave boy," my mom told me, holding me around my shoulders and searching for my eyes. "And you have grown into a wonderful young man."

I pondered something aloud that I had never considered. "Where were you that night? Lexi was with our neighbor, and you were gone."

My mom flushed. She searched for an answer and came up short. Finally, she pulled away from me, embarrassed. "I don't remember," she lied.

I waited for her to speak again, but when she did, she said, "You were lucky that you weren't killed."

"I couldn't save him," I said lamely.

"Would you have wanted me to save him?" Lexi asked. She had been hiding in the hallway, listening to our conversation. "I'm the same age you were when it happened."

Already forgiven for her transgression, she climbed into my lap and hung her arms loosely around my neck. I put my chin on her head and breathed in the scent from her strawberry children's shampoo.

"Razz has survivor's guilt," our mom said. "There was nothing he could do, but he feels as though he should have suffered in some way, even though his father was protecting him."

He might still be alive if I hadn't been there for him to protect, I thought. I was reluctant to say anything more in front of my sister.

"There's nothing he could have done," my mom repeated, as if reading my thoughts. "Your father was camping in an area that was thick with wildlife. A mother bear may have seen him as a danger to her cubs."

My mom gave us a little clear soda. She considered it a treat, since we weren't allowed to have caffeine or products with heavy sugar, so we drank it gratefully.

Lexi's head bobbed against my chest before it came to rest on my collarbone. My mom moved to wake her, but I lifted my sister easily and carried her to her fluffy bed. I stood over her a moment, watching her easy breaths and wondering how different her life would have been if our father had stayed.

It wasn't always perfect, but we were a harmonious household. My mom and dad loved each other, even though my mom didn't like to talk about him after he left.

I hugged my mom and slumped to my room. Occasional sobs shook my body, the after-effects of the feelings I had shared with my mom.

I felt in my pocket for the vial that I had taken from Monique's drawer, but my hands only found dusty particles and tiny shards. Lexi must have broken the vial when she sat on my lap!

I carefully slid off my jeans and found a piece of notebook paper. I painstakingly emptied my pocket until I had preserved almost all the contents of the vial. I darted to the kitchen for a sandwich bag, and placed the remaining dust, notebook paper included, into it. I sealed the bag and hid it inside the pocket of a robot jacket that I had worn when I was Lexi's age. I vowed to bring the bag with me whenever I left the house until I decided to use it.

I took the broken vial to the bathroom with me and wrapped it in toilet paper. I sent the broken glass into the town's sewers.

I turned my television on a familiar comedy and flung myself onto the bed. I tried to tune out the world and sleep, but I kept pulling myself back to the talk I'd had with my mom.

Several things about the conversation stuck out to me. I hadn't thought my father acted delusional, but I had seen the needle marks on his arms. I wished that I could say that he wasn't on drugs, but I was unsure. *Could that have been the real reason we were breaking into houses?*

A memory flashed, making me certain my father hadn't been on drugs. I had found a drawer full of pills and money at a house. He had rinsed the pills down the sink and closed the drawer with the money still inside it.

Maybe he took another type of drug, my brain whispered. *After all, he didn't throw away that vial you gave him.*

I tried to shake the thought from my mind, and I rested on another troubling part of my conversation with my mom. Where was she on the night my father died?

She had brushed off my question. She wasn't willing to tell me what she was doing that night. How could I find out about it? I could read her diary, but it would be an extreme breach of trust.

Maybe it didn't matter where my mom was that night anyway, I thought as I drifted off to sleep. But even in the twilight haze of my fading consciousness, I knew that it did.

CHAPTER TWENTY-SIX

I twirled a pencil casually over my fingers while Aiden dumped a bunch of words on me at one time. I peered over my glasses at him, to show some interest, but not too much.

"My dad came back from Japan this weekend," he started. "We went to the racetrack, and he knows a lot of people. I might go with him when he leaves next time."

I kept a casual demeanor, even though I was worried about my friend's safety. "Where are you going?"

Aiden took a minute to answer, and his excitement had lessened. "Probably New Zealand. But maybe Australia. I don't know."

I nodded my head slowly. It really wasn't my business anyway. "So, you and your dad are cool now."

Aiden didn't like the turn the conversation had taken. "It's fine," he grumbled.

The start of class kept us from testing the limits of the already uncomfortable conversation. Mr. Fritz's voice drowned out all other sounds, and the monotony of it pushed me into a doze.

When the bell rang, I lifted my chin off my chest and wiped the drool off my mouth. I acclimated to the commotion of papers shuffling and the roller coaster volume of voices, but my eyes wouldn't focus. I shut them tightly, moving them back and forth behind my lids, and reopened them, but I couldn't see the fine lines of people and objects. I frantically pulled my glasses off and rubbed my eyes.

"Are you okay?" Loila's voice lilted.

Startled by her proximity, I jumped, and my eyes flashed open.

I had looked longingly at Loila over the last several years, memorizing her dimples, blue eyes, and glorious blond hair. Everything about her was the same, but it was brought into hyper attention. Her dimples pushed deeper into her skin, leaving the mark of their potential, even when her face was relaxed. Her eyes were cerulean, with starbursts from the iris, and I could almost count the number of hairs that lined the arch over her eyes.

"Razz, are you okay?" Loila repeated.

"Yeah," I responded automatically, still dazed by my new perception.

I put my glasses back on and everything became fuzzy. My eyes hurt from trying to blink the desks and moving students into focus. I took off my glasses and the world slipped back into a surreal view.

"That must have been a powerful nap," Loila remarked.

I smiled in agreement and walked with her to our second class.

I couldn't look at the floor. Every step rushed up to meet me, like I was walking on the top of a bubble. I listened to Loila talk about shopping for a dress for the banquet as I took in everything around me. I was mesmerized by the pores in the drop ceiling and enchanted by the lines on the walls. I stopped at a locker to appreciate the chips in the metal. "Would you say this is more flaxen or corn colored?" I joked. My newfound ability had put me in an unusually good humor.

Loila quickly recovered, but she flashed a look of concern before she asked, "Razz, are you colorblind?"

Her question rocked me, but I shrugged my shoulders and relaxed into my usually cool demeanor. "I never thought about it."

"The lockers are green," Loila whispered. Her eyebrows moved together, and she added, "We've never really talked about colors, have we?"

"That's not really a conversation people have," I laughed.

"True," Loila agreed. "But I've asked you if a skirt looks cute, or if you like my shirt, and you always say 'yes.' You never talk about the color."

She stopped abruptly as if she were struck by inspiration. "What color is your mom's hair?" I knew it was a trick question, but I answered honestly. "It's brown."

"Ha!" Loila called out, surprising a group of clucking girls. They ran off giggling. "Your mom's hair is auburn," she declared.

"Okay," I accepted. "But auburn is like a brown-red."

"Can you see the red in it, though?" she asked, moving her eyebrows up and down.

Loila had busted me on a technicality, and she knew it. She practically danced into Monique's classroom.

"What's up with her?" Monique asked after Loila passed her.

"Apparently, I'm colorblind," I chuckled, "and she was the first person to point it out to me."

"Did you break your glasses?"

"No," I answered, holding them up for her to inspect. "I went to sleep in my first class, and I could see better when I woke up."

"You can't see the board without your glasses," she stated, obviously mistaking my honest answer for a joke.

I searched the room for an example to prove myself. I settled on a test paper that hung on the far wall. I recited Tabitha's well-written answers completely.

I don't know what kind of reaction I was expecting from Monique, but her look of deep contemplation surprised me. As a scientist, my condition may have been of some interest to her. She didn't comment, so I left her to ponder whatever had crossed her mind.

Monique was halfway through a lecture about telomeres when it hit me. I had *touched* the Scorn dust when I moved it from my pocket to the paper and into the bag. *Had I breathed it in?*

The possibility that the drug had entered my body and infected my bloodstream seemed logical. After all, it had been rumored that most people who had taken Scorn had snorted it into their noses. *Had I been careful enough to prevent rogue pieces of the swirling embers of dust from entering my nose or mouth?*

I tried to brush away my fear, but when I thought about my acute vision, I prayed that the amount in my bloodstream wasn't enough to cause the horrible side effects.

I tried to console myself. *Most users don't show signs of aggression until they have taken it a few times.*

I hoped that Monique's contemplation hadn't been over my newfound sense and the vial she had believed was still in her drawer. When the class concluded, she opened the drawer and confirmed her suspicion. I tried to avoid her stare, but my unwillingness to meet her eyes only confirmed my guilt.

I had to think fast, and I didn't know if I could talk myself out of this one.

CHAPTER TWENTY-SEVEN

Classroom couples lined up to discuss the reason that they were the best choice for Cutest Class Couple. The decision would be made by popular vote on the night of the event, but sometime in previous years the couples who had endeared themselves to each other the longest would present speeches to persuade the students to vote in their favor.

Three couples had chosen to stand in front of the sixty or so eighth graders in their class. Johnny Wade and Lily Vest presented the final scene of Romeo and Juliet. It moved most of the girls to cry, but I cringed at their melodrama. Chase Wilson and Melinda Hughes spoke about their relationship from the moment they met in third grade until the unique way he asked her to the banquet. Gregory Smith shocked everyone when he got down on one knee in a mock proposal to Bethany Wells.

I could feel Monique's eyes on me. I tried to pretend like I was laughing with Loila, or goofing off with Aiden, but part of me was dreading the inevitable conversation that I was going to have with my mom's best friend.

The assembly ended and I bolted to my next class. I thought I was safe, but Monique peeked around the corner. She asked my teacher if she could speak to me in the hallway.

Monique faced me and I waited for her judgement. "We have to talk about it," she said simply. "If we don't do it here then I'll have to go to your house after school." She placed her hands on her hips. "How do you want to do it?"

"I need to finish my test in this class," I lied, hedging for more time.

Monique's eyes bore into me, peeling the layers of my fabrication away. I was almost ready to go ahead and talk it out with her when she said, "Fine. I'll see you after school."

She turned on her heel and walked away, leaving me to wonder if it had been best to put off her accusations. *Would I really have an excuse ready by the time school was over?*

I resumed my seat in class and pondered possible loopholes. *Could I tell her that I thought it was colored sugar she had confiscated from a student?* No. Pictures of Scorn were everywhere to increase awareness, and the vials and their colored contents were public knowledge.

My teacher stopped pointedly after writing a formula. It was our clue to write it down in our notes. When I looked up, I spied Rowan staring at me. She glanced at the teacher to be certain that his back was turned and threw me a piece of notebook paper folded in a football shape. I caught it and pulled it open in stages, so I didn't arouse suspicion.

It was uncommon for people to pass notes anymore, but Rowan didn't have a way to send me a message on my phone. After some kids had tagged me in posts about killer bears and people who killed bears, I had made all my accounts private. She had asked me for my phone number, but I had pretended that I was in a hurry to avoid hurting her feelings. I didn't trust her, but it was best for her to believe I did.

The note read: *My sister is making me decorate the venue for the banquet. Can you help?*

Instead of writing a response, I waited for Rowan to look my way. I nodded slightly. She flashed a perfectly white smile.

It was a perfectly timed excuse. Monique and I would have a discussion eventually, but it wouldn't be after school today.

CHAPTER TWENTY-EIGHT

"It's uneven," Rowan observed when I finished hanging balloons.

I bit my cheek to keep from responding to her comment. I thought of several snide remarks, but I decided to keep them to myself.

"Oh, it's not your fault," she said to me, placing her hand on my arm. I purposely dropped a balloon and picked it up, slipping away from her touch.

"Madison!" Rowan called.

A girl with a smooth complexion and brown wavy hair bounced up to us. "Hey, Ro," she smiled. "What's up?"

"Rowan," Rowan corrected, and then addressed the decorations that I had hung. "The balloons aren't the same size, so it throws off the balance."

"It's impossible to make them *exactly* the same size," Madison said a little too brightly.

"Then tell your balloon monkeys to at least make them *around* the same size," Rowan shot back.

Madison stomped away, but she spoke to the girls in charge of the balloons. She threw eye daggers at Rowan, but Rowan continued to stare at the decorations, unaware of Madison's hostility.

"Is Madison your sister?" I asked.

Rowan had been lost in thought and she jumped when I spoke. Her eyebrows drew together. "No," she spat.

I looked around at the other people on the decoration committee. Aside from the last-minute recruits, like Aiden, Rowan, and me, most of the volunteers were cheerleaders. I wondered which one of them was Rowan's sister. I scanned a few faces, but none of them shared similar features. That didn't mean anything, though. Most of the people I knew who had a sibling looked different from them. Very few people had a brother or sister who looked as much alike as Lexi and me.

Rowan bit her nail, and I noticed her hand. My breath caught in my throat before all the heat of my emotions flooded my face. *She was wearing the emerald ring I had gotten Loila for her birthday!*

"Where did you get that ring?" I asked her. I felt like I was breathing the words through fire, but my question came out evenly.

Maddeningly, Rowan smirked. "You finally noticed? I wore it at the party. Loila even complimented me on it."

I tried to reign in my anger, but I could feel fiery splotches on my face and neck. "It's *Loila's* ring."

She held her hand out arm's length and admired it. "It looks better on me, don't you think?" I resisted the urge to forcefully pull the ring off her finger. She dangled it under my nose. "After I saw the way you threw the box on the gift table, I knew you wouldn't mind."

I had been embarrassed from my awkward exchange with Loila when I had tossed the gift onto the table and run outside. I didn't try to explain my actions to Rowan. Instead, I stood there, hoping she'd give me the ring.

When it was clear that she wouldn't get the desired outburst from me, Rowan rolled her eyes. "You're no fun," she declared, and slipped the ring off her hand. I grabbed it and pushed it into my pocket.

"Still friends?" she said.

I wanted to tell her, 'No!' and spit all the curse words I knew at her, but there was still something that drew me to her. For some reason, Rowan was supposed to be in my life, and I needed to find out if she was a spy for the underground Scorn ring, or simply a piece in an even larger puzzle.

Mrs. Holt breezed into the room and announced that the pizzas had arrived. The mention of food in a room full of teenagers created a buzz that made a response from me unnecessary.

"That's the best part about doing this," Aiden said as he rushed past us. The line was too long by the time he got there, so he fell back and stood with Rowan and me. Within minutes, we sat in a circle in the room's farthest corner. Rowan had negotiated an entire pizza for us.

"I hope you guys like meat," she said, opening the box. She had cut the line and unceremoniously swiped the pizza. There were several angry looks thrown at her, but no one called her out. My mouth watered at the sight of pepperoni, sausage, bacon, and hamburger. I had to hold myself back from grabbing half of it.

"They slaughtered a pig and tossed in a little cow for fun," Aiden joked while he chewed. Rowan winced when she saw the food dance in his mouth, but I was used to it. Aiden never stopped talking. "I'm glad I let you talk me into this," he said to me, tearing a bite from a slice that drooped in his hand. His next words were surrounded by gooey cheese and seasoned meat. "I'm in a oom full a girlth and food."

Rowan glared at him. I held up my pizza in his direction in a gesture of good cheer and folded the meaty slice into my mouth.

"Do all boys eat like pigs?" Rowan asked, staring at me in disgust.

"Only the good ones," Aiden answered, chomping noisily.

My phone buzzed, and I stared at the message on my screen without accessing it. I didn't want my mom to know that I had read it.

"Was it your mom?" Aiden asked when we broke off from Rowan. "Did Monique tell her what we did?"

"Yes," I answered. Aiden didn't know that my mom had already talked to me about our experience in Monique's classroom, but he was completely unaware of the vial I took from our teacher's drawer. I wanted to keep it that way.

"I'd hate to be you when you get home," he chuckled.

I thought of Monique standing beside my mom as she tapped her foot. "You have no idea."

I decided to answer the message, and when I clicked on it the entirety of the message was revealed. I was relieved to see that Monique had been there, but she said that she would talk to me on the morning after the dance.

"I gotta bounce," I told Rowan and Aiden.

"Is it your mom?" Aiden called after me.

I nodded and threw up two fingers. I felt a little guilty about leaving right after eating the pizza, but I had been there for a while, and everything seemed to be decorated.

When I got home, my mom wasn't standing next to the door, but she had sent Lexi to her room in anticipation of my return. I casually strutted down the hall until she said, "I need to talk to you."

I drifted into the living room. "What's up?"

My mom was seated on our couch with her legs resting across it. She moved into a sitting position and patted the seat beside her. We were a little too close for a conversation about my thievery.

"Why was Monique here?" she asked me.

My mind stopped looping around potential explanations, but I kept my relief from showing in my features. "She's *your* friend," I answered. "Why didn't you ask her?"

My mom set her jaw. "She said she was here to see *you*," she managed through clenched teeth. She was tired more often, and it caused brief lapses in her patience. She relaxed her posture and submitted to her emotional exhaustion. "Why does it seem like I'm purposely being kept in the dark? You know that I hate to be blind-sided."

"No one is trying to keep anything from you," I lied. I draped my arm lazily over her shoulders. She settled into me, unwilling to argue when our time together was limited.

After a few moments she asked, "Are you going to be okay, Razzberry?"

"Yeah, I'm fine."

"No," she persisted. "I mean are you okay with the way I have chosen to die?"

"Well, I guess I kinda have to be," I answered honestly.

My mom lifted up to face me. "Don't you think a person should choose the way they want to die if they have a terminal illness?"

"Sure, Mom," I spoke agreeably. "I'll be okay."

"You think I'm being selfish," my mom observed. She closed her eyes tightly and reopened them quickly. "But you don't have to throw up after chemotherapy and watch your body go through unimaginable changes."

"Aren't you doing that anyway? You still throw up and lose weight."

My mom considered my words. "But the medicine hurt me."

"The cancer is eating you away," I responded. "Doesn't it hurt worse?"

My mom buried her head in her hands. "It's already overtaken me!" she exclaimed, throwing up her hands. "What am I supposed to do? Postpone the inevitable?"

My mom was getting upset and I didn't want to deal with her emotional outburst. "It's fine, Mom," I tried. "You can choose the way you way you die. I'll be okay."

"No you won't," my mom cried. "I know what it's like to lose a mother, and it's so hard."

I patted her leg. "Everything will be okay," I told her again. I got up to make a speedy escape.

"You look more like him every day," my mom croaked, stopping me before I could retreat into my room.

"Like Dad?" I questioned, even though I knew who she meant.

"Yes. You have his eyes," she replied with a half-smile. "And his bushy hair," she added. She dropped her eyes and lowered her voice. "He used to leave when I got upset, too."

I felt her words like a punch to my gut. I decided to ignore them. "Just don't do the same to Lexi," she finished before I snaked down the hall.

CHAPTER TWENTY-NINE

I wasn't going to go to the banquet. I had decided to stay in my room and stare at the ceiling weeks ago, so I hadn't made plans to find a date or tuxedo. My mom felt differently.

She and Lexi burst into my room at ten o'clock, an absolutely disrespectful hour. They opened my curtains and brilliant sunlight flooded the room.

I rolled onto my side and curled into a fetal position. I had kicked my blankets onto the floor, but I grabbed a pillow to block the sun from my eyes. Lexi tugged at my pillow, but I was able to hold it firmly over my head.

"It's time to get ready," my mom chirped.

I tried to ignore her. Maybe they would get tired of waiting on me and go on their own.

"Let's go, Razzberry," she pressed.

"Where?"

"Your suit is ready," she told me.

"What?" I sighed, but I already knew. My mom filled me in on her plan, and I pieced together that she had made arrangements for me before she finished telling me about them.

I sat up and Lexi snapped a picture on our mom's phone. She flashed the screen in front of my face so that I could see my unruly hair and hateful expression.

"I'm not going to the dance," I affirmed.

"I was thinking about that," my mom intoned. "It's a banquet, not a dance, so there's a little more meaning to it. After you helped with the decorations yesterday, I knew that you were more excited about it than you let on."

My mom thought she only needed to give me a push to go to the banquet. I really had no interest in dancing or talking to the people I had to see at school five days a week on a Saturday night while I was dressed in a suit that felt like it had me in a chokehold.

"My friend, Hannah, had three suits left at her store, and I picked the best one for you," my mom squealed. "You remember Hannah," she prompted. "She used to hike with us when Lexi was little."

My mom had found a way around mentioning that Hannah had not hiked with us since my father had died. I remembered that Hannah used to give me a peppermint after every mile we hiked. I used to watch the trail signs so that I could hold my hand out for my special treat.

"Well deserved," she would say when she handed one to me. She would have me recall what I noticed each mile, like which birds were out, or if there were trees fallen along the path.

"That's nice, Mom, but I'm not going," I said firmly. I didn't want to hurt her feelings, but she was starting to irritate me. "I would have gotten a suit if I would have wanted to go."

My mom's smile faltered, but she pasted it back on her face. "Then we're going out to a late lunch," she continued. "You didn't ask Loila to the dance, so you can dine with your two favorite ladies." She grinned at Lexi, and my sister jumped up and down.

"Mom said we can go wherever you want, except Bones," she giggled.

Bones was famous for its expensive meat buffet. I had joked about taking my mom there since she had forced her vegetarian diet on us.

Lexi started dancing around my room. She picked up my dragon lamp and pretended to polish it. She twirled past my television, getting tangled in a pile of my shirts and almost knocking my gaming system off my dresser.

"Hey, stop," I commanded. "You're going to get hurt."

"Your brother's right. Go finish getting ready."

Lexi hopped out of the room, flicking one of my old soft-bullet guns from under the bed with her foot.

"I'll leave so you can get ready," my mom said, patting my knee.

"I'm not going," I repeated. I tried to laugh it off and stay in a good humor.

My mom stood with her back to me. After a moment, she pushed my door shut. When she sat back down on my bed, there were tears in her eyes.

"Razzberry," she choked. She cleared her throat and blinked her eyes several times. One tear escaped, and she wiped it away quickly. "I'm not going to get to see you for your senior prom."

I hadn't thought about it from my mom's perspective. She had just put in the paperwork to leave her teaching position. Her oncologist had told her not to make plans to teach the next school year.

"I'm not going to see you on your wedding day," she went on. Her face was wet with emotion, even though she kept wiping it with her shirt sleeve. "Please let me do this for you."

I was ready to argue my point. I had every reason to stay home, and if my mom had wanted me to go to the banquet so badly then she should have said something about it months ago. She worked in the same school, so she saw the flyers and event posters.

There was something different in the way she asked me, though. It was fragile and more complex than her sadness over missed future formal events. She wanted to share the experience with me and be part of the memory I had of the banquet. She didn't want to be lost in a file of faded photographs and half-forgotten family nights.

I let out a long sigh. "Does Hannah still have peppermints?"

CHAPTER THIRTY

I stood in front of the mirror and admired my reflection. I felt like a penguin in a bright white shirt with a black pair of pants and jacket with tails.

"Absolutely perfect!" my mom squealed.

Hannah raised her eyebrows at the floor and busied herself with a dress my sister had discarded. Hannah had seemed to have more in common with my dad than my mom, so it wasn't a surprise that we hadn't seen her since he died.

After I changed, I ran my hand across a couple of silk suits. I stopped when I heard my mom arguing with Hannah.

"But I want to pay you for it!" she insisted in a whisper.

Hannah's voice remained low and even. I could only make out the difference in the tone of her speech and the sharp refusal it conveyed.

I decided to intervene. As I had expected, my presence caused the women to stop squabbling.

"There he is!" my mom beamed.

"You are a handsome boy," Hannah complimented. She handed me a fake monocle to complete my look and two peppermints.

I tried to give Lexi one of them, but Hannah stopped me. "I will give the sprite a treat. You must eat one now, and one at the prom."

"Banquet," my mom corrected. "He's only in eighth grade."

Hannah pulled the stillness from the room into her posture and stared unwaveringly at my mom. "Of course," she seethed.

I tried to think of a way to improve the situation. "Why do you give me peppermints?" I asked.

"The mint helps spark your mind to make a memory," Hannah answered simply.

"Maybe I should give them to my class before a test," my mom laughed uneasily. She wasn't used to being a pariah, and she was still trying to win over Hannah's favor.

"Only if you give them peppermints during the lessons. Do you have trouble conveying elementary material properly?" Hannah quipped.

I rescued my mom from further hostility and guided her out the door. I looked back at Hannah, but she turned her back to me to pull something out of a glass case. I dropped the peppermints into my pocket

"Why is she mean to you?" Lexi asked our mom when we left the shop.

"I think she had a crush on your father," my mom sighed. "They knew each other long before he met me."

"Didn't she have a husband?" I remembered. A bald man with a guitar had always struggled to keep pace with her on our hikes. I thought the guitar he carried weighed him down, and I remembered that his shoulder bones made prominent peaks out of his shirt.

"Lionel," my mom nodded. "They're still married, but I don't think Hannah was with anyone until your father married me."

I spotted a food truck and ran for it. My sister followed, trying to catch me. My mom had wanted to sit down in a restaurant, but I preferred to go to food trucks. You could find them anywhere in the county next to the road or tucked into a street next to a popular business. I was amazed by the people who owned the trucks. They always treated you as if you were their favorite customer and they were eager to tell their stories.

My favorite food truck, Smokin' Hot, was parked in an empty lot behind an old bank building. The owners, Henry and Nettie, were from the area, and they decided to buy an old truck and sell barbeque when their youngest of five children left for college.

"Did you go to the free fishin' day for kids?" Henry asked when he saw Lexi out of breath behind me.

"Nah," I replied. "I picked up a suit for the banquet."

"I always felt like a monkey in 'em," he commented. "I put one on fer my prom, but Nettie didn't make me wear one fer our weddin'."

At the mention of her name, Nettie appeared, tossing a damp hand towel over her shoulder. The smoked meat they made kept her warm, and perspiration beaded her forehead.

"I remember my first dance," she smiled. "Floyd Byrd spilled punch on my dress and then threw up on me."

Henry and I gave her a quizzical look. Lexi voiced our question. "Why are you smiling about it?"

"It meant that I was so pretty that I made him nervous," she answered, winking at my sister before she slipped away from the window.

Lexi and I picked the same meat sandwich, loaded with pulled pork. My mom paid for our food without adding to the order. Henry didn't tease her about putting meat on her bones, like he had months ago. Everyone could tell that my mom's weight loss was because of the invisible beast that drained her every day.

We ate our meal at the park next to the library. Lexi abandoned most of her sandwich to play on the slide before I was done with my food. My mom stared into the breeze that picked up her hair and swirled around her face. I wondered if she thought it felt like my dad's hands caressing her cheeks.

"I'm on top of the world!" Lexi announced, standing on the bar above the slide. My mom broke from her peace and bolted to one side of the slide, and I rushed to the other, but Lexi jumped onto the slide and ran down it.

"That's not what slides are for," my mom scolded.

My sister looked at me like we shared a secret, so I knew that I needed to say something. "Hey, you could have broken your arm again."

Lexi rolled her eyes and shrugged off our warnings.

My mom didn't make Lexi finish her sandwich, and she threw it away. Our meal cost our mom more than she would admit, but she would rather bring peanut butter sandwiches to work for a week than carry the meat through our door.

"Can I go to the library?" Lexi begged. She loved to read on the platform 9 3/4 station they had constructed in the teen room.

"Not today," our mom said. "We need to go home so your brother can get ready for his banquet."

To my horror, Monique was there when we got home. My sister danced around her, telling her about our day in one long, run-on sentence.

Monique stopped me before I could slink away. "I'm not going to ruin your day," she assured me. "This means a lot to your mom. But tomorrow, we're going to talk."

I nodded my understanding and spent a long part of the afternoon trimming my nails, showering, and fixing my hair. My mom offered her styling products, and I used her mousse to help my waves flow without flyaways.

I posed for a couple of pictures, even though I found it ridiculous. Lexi and my mom had dressed up, and we all drove out to a covered bridge on the other end of the county. I humored my mom by taking several pictures alone and with Lexi and her, but it was hot, and I was starting to sweat.

"Can we wrap this up?" I asked.

My mom was crestfallen, but she agreed that I needed to get to the banquet. "Take one with Monique," she pressed, plucking the phone out of her friend's hand.

Monique was just as surprised as me, but she threw her arm naturally around me. Lexi squeezed into a couple of the pictures, and my mom made one of them her phone's screen saver.

"My family," she mused before Monique reminded her that I needed to get to the banquet.

I piled into the car with them, and I reflected on my mom's words. Monique was a part of our family, but I had never considered how much of my life she had been present for until that moment. I begrudgingly admitted to myself that she had been around more than my father. I watched her joke with my mom about the music on the radio, and I could almost feel the connection that they shared. Lexi and I were losing our mom, and Monique was losing her closest friend. I wondered what it meant to her and how it would change her.

My family was the center of my universe, and my mom was the sun. What would happen to Lexi, Monique, and me when her warmth and light was gone?

CHAPTER THIRTY-ONE

The eighth-grade banquet took place at a venue just off Main Street. My mom pulled our car as close as she could get to the throng of eighth graders lined up on the sidewalk and parked in the courthouse parking lot. She insisted on walking me to the door, but Monique stopped her before we made it to a huge crowd of kids gathered at the entrance.

"I don't have a ticket!" I realized.

"I took care of it," Monique said, passing me a bright white slip of paper with green filigree.

"One more picture," my mom begged.

I let her snap a photo of me in my most famous pose —with my index and middle fingers out on each hand —and one with Lexi and me. I pretended to look at the pictures when she gushed over my formal appearance.

"Don't you always chaperone the banquets?" I ask Monique.

"I passed on that this year. I spend five days a week with you, I don't need you crashing my weekend, too."

Our banter amused Lexi, and she stopped balancing on the curb to listen.

"Yeah, okay," I laughed, mousing Monique's hair playfully. She made a token attempt to bat my hand away, but she let me get the best of her. "Then don't be there when I get home."

"Not a chance," came her swift reply. She winked, and we all laughed. I hugged each of them and joined the crowd at the door.

I waited on couples with bright white and baby blue dresses and suits—colors that would show up well under the black lights—to step into the cool one-room venue. The boys awkwardly placed their sweaty hands on the middle of their dates' backs to escort them into the banquet.

The seventh graders had chosen the theme of our dance and they had arranged a glow party for us. I had helped place the blacklights, so I avoided the areas of the room that would project the white in my teeth and shirt. Freckles, tanning inconsistencies, and dental work stood out in the room, but most of the students were unaware of their spotlighted flaws.

The room buzzed with activity, but no one was dancing. To my left, the town's favorite photographer flashed photographs of smiling girls and uncertain boys, who placed shaking hands on the shoulders of their dates. I could smell food in the back of the room, but only a few kids filled a plate. Most people were scared to spill cheese dip or punch on their fine clothes.

A DJ tried to interact with the growing crowd. Some of the kids were yelling for him to play some controversial songs, while a few others were calling for funny ones. I heard someone shout out the name of a well-known pre-school tune, and I traced the sound of the voice to Aiden.

Aiden and Rowan were already at a table. Aiden was chomping tortilla chips, and Rowan was wishing she had remained unescorted to the banquet. Aiden seemed oblivious to her body language. He yelled out "Chicken Dance," and Rowan crossed her legs away from him, put her elbow on the table, and placed the side of her head in her hand. She was more mature than her classmates, and I wondered what had happened to make her that way.

"How're ya doin', Old Sport?" he yelled to me over the music. He had used a mock English accent, and I was almost inclined to return it, but I held my cool demeanor. "Tails?" he commented.

I turned around so he could get the full effect.

"Where's your top hat?" Rowan smirked.

I pulled a monocle out of my pocket and inched it onto my cheek. Aiden and Rowan burst into hysterics.

"Very cute," Mrs. Holt said behind me.

I bowed and offered her my hand. "Have fun guys," she chuckled, and moved away without accepting my gesture.

Rowan rolled her eyes.

"What happened with you and Mrs. Holt?" Aiden asked.

"*Stephanie* doesn't know how to mind her own business," she snapped.

"It's *Stephanie* now," Aiden emphasized.

"I thought you weren't coming to the banquet?" Rowan said. She narrowed her eyes, but she didn't seem angry. She crossed her arms and pretended to pout.

My eyes followed the low cut of Rowan's purple dress. It would have been too revealing for a teenager if not for the tulle around the bust that puffed like freshly whipped icing. I noted a severely raised scar that capped her shoulder and upper arm. I hadn't observed it at Loila's party when she took off her shirt, but I had been standing on her other side when we had talked that day.

"Nice dress," I complimented.

Aiden noticed me looking at the puffy material around her chest and raised his eyebrows, and I quickly diverted my attention. I was feeling bolder than usual, but I didn't want Rowan for myself.

"Thank you," she responded genuinely. "I designed it."

I nodded agreeably when she got up and modeled the way the satin spun around her knees. She sat back down and waited for Aiden's praise, but he wasn't paying attention.

"Loila's here," Rowan remarked casually. Her back was to the door, but Loila breezed into the room when she spoke.

"How did you know?"

"You can smell her perfume a mile away," she replied, waving away my question.

Loila entered arm-in-arm with Tabitha, and they stopped at the camera for photos. I was drawn to her cheerful dimples and carefree smile. I stood three feet away before I realized that I had left Aiden and Rowan.

Loila's dress spun in brilliant whites and pinks that reflected the blacklights. Her french manicure popped, and it almost made me dizzy when I watched her, as she always moved her hands when she spoke.

She spotted me and drew me in to a quick hug. Rowan was right: I could smell her soft jasmine scent.

I pretended to shield my eyes. "White and pink?" I asked about her dress.

She looked down at the reflection of the lights on her gown. "Actually, it's two different shades of white."

"It's weird how things show up in the blacklight." I smiled, hoping all my teeth were the same color under the unforgiving light.

The DJ had finally given in, and the lyrics of "Baby Shark" assaulted our ears. No one really danced anymore, aside from some of the online dances that internet personalities made up, but a few of the students had started a conga line in the center of the room. The DJ realized the way to gain audience approval and played the requests the silly young teens threw out at him. Loila and Tabitha grabbed my hands, and we joined the group for "What Does the Fox Say?"

I hardly moved, except to walk behind Loila with my hands on her bare shoulders. Her hair had been professionally fixed, and diamonds and small braids wove through it in a half-swirl pattern. Loila moved with a freedom I hadn't seen in months. Her laughter was more musical than anything the DJ could have played. I wished that I would have asked her to go to the banquet with me, and I daydreamed about the food, pictures, and embarrassment over our parents' gushing that we didn't experience together.

Aiden dragged Rowan to the dance floor, but she pulled away after half a song. I wondered why she didn't want to participate, since she had been talking about the banquet for months. She went back to the table and tapped her foot, like she couldn't wait for the night to end.

We wound around the room wildly for half an hour. The DJ played a slow song, and Loila raised her eyebrows at me. Surprisingly, Aiden had asked Tabitha to dance, and Tabitha was lost in his casual hold. Aiden looked around the room, probably to locate Rowan, found her, and settled into a moment with Tabitha.

Loila had followed my gaze. "Poor Tabitha. She really likes Aiden, but he's only dancing with her to make Rowan jealous."

"Yeah, and Rowan only went to the dance with him because I told her that I wasn't going."

"What changed your mind?"

"My mom," I answered. By this point, we had gotten past the awkward moment where I was supposed to ask her to dance, and we moved away from the stiffly moving couples to the oversized punch bowl.

"Can I get you some punch?" I offered.

"I can grab it," Loila laughed. "But thank you."

I felt ridiculous for asking her. We each picked up a punch cup and drank greedily. Dancing had dehydrated us.

Mrs. Holt's student aide stood sentinel beside the punch bowl. She refilled new plastic cups as others were lifted by students.

"Why aren't you guys dancing?" she called to us.

Loila looked at me when she answered, "He didn't ask me."

I almost spit punch out onto my rented suit. I coughed a little and searched for the words that would save me from further embarrassment. I came up with nothing.

"Shame on you," the teacher's aide mock scolded. "You'll have to make that up to her when they play another slow song."

Loila smiled and my mouth went dry, despite the cup of punch I had just gulped. The song ended, and Aiden bounced up to me, saving me from an awkward commitment.

"Where's Rowan?" he asked.

I glanced in the direction of the table, but she wasn't there anymore. "Maybe she went to the bathroom."

"She's not in there," Kelly said, gliding up to our group. "I was just in there with the rest of our squad. She looked pointedly at Loila. "Where were you?"

Loila's countenance darkened. "I told you that I quit."

Kelly almost cackled with forced laughter. "I'll tell you when you're done," she lilted. She moussed Loila's hair, and a couple of the fake diamonds fell from the style. "It's time."

The rest of the squad gathered around Loila, and I heard a shriek. I spotted Rowan on the other side of the room arguing with Mrs. Holt. Most of the room watched the scene, but I turned back, ready to defend Loila.

Loila and the cheerleading squad were gone. I scanned the room for them, but I didn't see any of them.

"Where did they go?" I asked Aiden, but he was still watching Rowan screech at Mrs. Holt.

"I'll go check the bathroom," Tabitha volunteered. I hadn't noticed her, but she had been hovering near Aiden.

When she came out and threw her hands up, I started asking the kids I knew if they had seen Loila. I was halfway through the crowd before a girl in exaggerated white glasses told me, "She left with the rest of the cheerleaders."

I grabbed Aiden and pulled him out the door. Orange and white barricades marked off a quarter of the street. The students could step outside for air, but the barricades were meant to act as a fence to keep us contained. A couple of teachers spoke warnings as we explored the edges of our constraints. I didn't see Loila anywhere.

"Where'd she go?" Aiden said.

Rowan stomped out of the door, fuming. "Augh!" she yelled into the night. One of the teachers scolded her outburst as Rowan stormed over to us.

"She can't even let me enjoy one night!" she shouted.

"Are you ever going to tell us what's up with you two?" Aiden tried.

Rowan shrugged him off. "Where's your little girlfriend?" she asked me.

"Loila and I aren't together," I managed to say smoothly. "We came out to look for her. She disappeared somewhere with the cheerleaders."

"She hardly *disappeared*," Rowan assured us. "They've taken her to complete the Rituals."

"What are they making her do?" I snapped, grabbing Rowan's arm. She looked at my hand on her arm and I dropped it. "Loila quit the squad."

"It doesn't matter if she quit," Rowan said inside a long sigh. "She started the Rituals. Now she has to finish them."

"What are they making her do?" I repeated.

"How am I supposed to know?" Rowan blazed. I thought I saw her eyes spark in the dark.

"You're friends with Kelly," Aiden countered. "You know *something*."

"I talk to Kelly at lunch," she dismissed. "No one else seems to enjoy my company, unless I can do something for them or be eye candy for an event." She eyed both of us individually as she spoke, and her expression appearing weathered by weathered a hundred storms.

"She's had to have said something, though," Aiden replied, missing Rowan's insinuations.

"That brat couldn't come up with a proper Ritual if her life depended on it," she spoke airily.

"Did you give Kelly an idea for Loila's Ritual?" I pushed.

"I didn't suggest ideas for anyone *specific*," she informed us haughtily. She ran her finger lazily down a plastic barrier. "I simply told her a story that happened a long time ago."

"Lost Cove?" I grabbed her shoulders before I knew it. A blast of heat rushed at me, causing perspiration to dot my face. I let her go, but we held each other's gaze.

"So what?" Rowan said. "Loila will spend one night tied up in an old, creaky house." She narrowed her eyes. "She may be even better for doing it."

I jumped the barrier without another thought. Aiden and Rowan must have followed me because I could hear the clicks of Rowans heels on the pavement. Teachers called after us, but their voices were drowned out by the blood marching through my ears.

I didn't stop until Rowan grabbed me. I was surprised by her strength, and I had to take long strides to stop, preventing a hard fall. I rounded on her.

"What are you going to do?" she shouted. "It would take you a day to get to Lost Cove on foot from here!"

I stared back at her. I wanted to turn around and keep running, but I had to admit she was right.

"I can get us a ride," she said softly. She took my silence for acceptance and dialed a number. She spoke quietly into the receiver and hung up quickly.

Aiden had been standing just beyond the sound of her voice. He limped up to me, wincing with each step. He had stumbled in his pursuit and hurt his ankle.

A dark blue sedan pulled up minutes later and we all climbed inside. Rowan rode in the front seat, and Aiden and I squeezed into the back next to a large bag of soccer balls.

"I double as the girls soccer coach," Mrs. Holt said when she saw us push against the bag.

Mrs. Holt was the last person I thought would agree to take us to Lost Cove. She was a teacher, and it went against a thousand school rules for her to take us anywhere, especially somewhere as potentially dangerous as Lost Cove.

"So, how long has it been since Kelly left with Loila," Mrs. Holt asked.

"About ten minutes," Rowan spat.

Mrs. Holt was doing her a favor, but Rowan acted as entitled as always. I had heard enough.

"Stop talking to her like that," I yelled at Rowan. "Mrs. Holt is helping us, but you're treating her like—"

"Whoa," Aiden spoke up. "Why don't we all just agree to get along until we find Loila."

"Fine by me," Mrs. Holt said.

I could almost hear Rowan roll her eyes. She crossed her arms and stared out the window.

I was so anxious about Loila that I didn't notice the miles slip away. Before I knew it, Mrs. Holt stopped the car.

The railroad tracks rolled out in front of us, and the overcast night hardly allowed moonlight to reach the gravel around the tracks. I was eager to get started, but Mrs. Holt made me wait on my friends.

Rowan pulled a bag out of Mrs. Holt's trunk. Mrs. Holt watched Aiden and me, even though we weren't thinking about looking at Rowan while she changed. We tried to make out any of their whispered conversation, but all we heard was "ATV."

I left my jacket in Mrs. Holt's car and added my shirt when Rowan handed Aiden and me two Pale Woods Academy sports shirts. The school's mascot, a buzzing yellow jacket, stood out from the bright yellow shirts. We could easily be seen, but we would preserve the top half of our tuxes.

Rowan was dressed in dark clothes, and I envied her tennis shoes. It was going to be hard for Aiden and me to run in our dress shoes.

Mrs. Holt pulled a bottle of water out for each of us. Between the ride, the team shirts, and the water, I was thankful she had been inside the car that had picked us up.

It was a twelve-mile hike to the ghost town, but the three of us ran like we tackled it every day. I wasn't surprised by Rowan's skill, but I was shocked that Aiden could keep up. I guessed one of the perks of being rich was that he had an array of exercise equipment in his home gym.

We ran the first two miles before Aiden held up his hand for us to stop. He collapsed onto the ground and pulled in sharp breaths of air while he held his side.

"They can't be that far ahead," he said between mouthfuls of air.

Rowan had jogged in place to keep her muscles warm while Aiden rested. "They took an ATV," she told him.

"You can smell the gas," I agreed.

Aiden gulped his bottle of water. It was almost gone when Rowan cautioned, "You only have one bottle of water, and you're not getting any of mine."

"Tsk, tsk," Aiden joked. "And after I gave you a ride to the banquet in a limo with a full juice bar." He signaled that he was ready to run again, and we rushed down the track.

I thought about Loila the entire time. I wondered how hard she had fought, and if she had managed to get away. I hoped we would see her running in our direction, but every mile was just as empty.

I had taken the lead and instinctively turned onto a small trail into the woods. We wound up the mountain for almost a half a mile until an open space emerged. I thought I heard a rattle once, but our pounding feet must have scared away snakes. Rowan jerked me back.

"Do you want them to see you?" she hissed.

I let Rowan scan the area. She closed her eyes and listened, letting the echoes of the cool breeze and rustling trees envelope her. When she motioned me to follow her, all her senses were heightened.

Aiden gasped for air and vomited into a bush. He was trying to be quiet, but the sounds of his retching echoed in the night.

"Let's go, Fairmont!" Rowan whispered. "Pick up the pace!"

Aiden made a garbled response that may have contained a few curses. Rowan ignored him and stepped carefully around the perimeter of the tree line.

In a few feet, I noticed an orange glow against the trees. We stayed hidden in some deep brush while we watched figures talk and laugh around the fire. Kelly's brother and one of his friends passed a bottle back and forth.

"They're gonna get mono," Aiden chomped.

Rowan rounded on him. "What's in your mouth!" she hissed.

Aiden smiled at her with bits of seed and berry flesh hanging between his teeth. "I found some berries."

Rowan swatted his hand and five berries fell onto the forest floor. She picked one up and studied it. "Blackberries," she confirmed.

"I knew that," Aiden said, but there was doubt in his voice.

"Why were you eating those after you just threw up?" she demanded.

"I had to get the taste out of my mouth," Aiden defended. "You told me that I couldn't drink my water."

"I wanted you to *conserve* your water, not eat random berries," Rowan fussed. "What if you had died?"

"Aww," Aiden cooed. "I didn't know you cared."

Rowan colored. "I'm just not going to carry your dead body off this mountain," she snapped.

"Stop," I interrupted. I pointed past them to the fire.

Kelly's brother and his friend cocked their heads and started walking in our direction. Along the way, one of them picked up a stick.

"We know you're there!" Kelly's brother shouted.

Rowan's eyes glinted. "It's me, Martin!" she called.

My breath caught in my throat and my mouth went dry. *Why had Rowan given up our position? How did she know Kelly's brother and his friend?*

She walked out of the shadows and waved. "Why did you bring Paul?"

"Morgan wanted him here," Kelly's brother shrugged.

"Are the initiates ready?" she questioned casually.

"The ones we brought are ready," Paul answered. "What about yours?"

"They're shaking like cowards behind those bushes."

"Come out, pups," Martin shouted at us. Paul added a cat call.

Aiden and I were frozen in place. I couldn't tell if revealing us was part of Rowan's plan to help us find Loila, or if I was in the middle of something bigger.

CHAPTER THIRTY - TWO

"Oh, come on," Rowan sighed, and pulled us both out of our hiding spots. Aiden and I stumbled into view, the crackling fire creating dances of light on our bright shirts.

"Aiden Fairmont and his little friend?" Paul chuckled.

"Yeah," Rowan agreed. "They started the turn last cycle."

"Are they the ones Beaux saw in the factory?" Martin asked, taking a drink from a lemony bottle.

"That's them," Rowan replied. "The bumbling idiots almost got themselves eaten."

"I have something to say," Aiden squeaked, raising his hand timidly. "What cycle?"

"Your menstrual cycle," Paul teased. "What do you think?"

"Your dad already talked to you," Rowan snapped. "Don't play dumb."

I had waited for a clearer explanation, but I only felt more confused. Finally, I had to admit defeat. "Where's Loila?"

"Let's take him to her," Paul chuckled, a sly grin inching up his face.

Aiden walked automatically, leaving me to wonder about his connection to the people who had taken our friend. I looked in his direction, but he kept his head down.

Lost Cove had once been a close-knit community, but little evidence remained of its inhabitants. A graveyard lay on a nearby hill, its markers like sporadic teeth in a yawning mouth. We dodged a truck, its paint rusting away and tall weeds growing through the bed. I let Rowan lead me up a stark hill to a white house. The interior was bathed with a battery-operated light, and the door was open. The walls held graffiti from years of secret teenage parties, but a large symbol stood out to me. A black ouroboros was intricately drawn on the wall facing the door, and it moved, inching across its place on the wall like the hands on a clock.

I saw Loila as soon as I stepped into the house. Her hands were bound behind her back, and the white and cream dress had been spoiled by dirt and grass stains. Kelly and two other girls stood over her, but the other two girls weren't on Pale Woods Academy's cheerleading squad. I didn't recognize them.

"Razz," Loila wheezed. She had screamed until her voice was hoarse.

"Let her go," I demanded.

"Oh, we will," Kelly giggled. The two other girls joined her mirth. "We'll untie her when you and your friend are ready."

Aiden looked miserable. In the bright light, the juice blackberries had left on his lip almost looked like blood.

"I thought that we were supposed to *protect* our friends," he tried.

"We do," Martin agreed. "But *she's* not one of us. *She's* food."

I had the feeling that I had stumbled into one of the most curious teenaged cults on this side of the east coast. I knew these kids. Well, most of them. I went to school with them. I had watched Aiden, Rowan, and Kelly eat bags of chips and doughnuts, but never people.

My mind raced to find a way out of the situation. I clawed for an explanation, but no one would tell me more than pieces that sounded like riddles to my uncomprehending brain.

"What do you want?" I asked.

"It's not what *we* want," Kelly answered. "It's what *she* wants." Loila struggled and sent spit flying at Kelly, but it only landed on her shoe. "Well, maybe I want it a little," she laughed, bending and shoving Loila's face onto the floor.

I jumped at Kelly to push her away from Loila, but Paul swatted me to the ground. I caught a glimpse of Aiden. His eyes shifted in my direction, but his head remained bowed. He wasn't going to help Loila or me.

"Enough!" Martin shouted. He seemed to be the oldest in the group and he was ready to take control. "We all agree that the initiates are close enough to full transformation?" He stared at his cohorts. Paul nodded and Kelly and the other two girls didn't object.

Martin clapped his hands together. "Okay then," he announced. "It's time to begin. Jessica, Kaitlyn, get your initiates."

As if on cue, two teens filtered in from another room. A girl, with dark hair and ivory skin held onto an athletic boy with a bright green shirt. He tried to help the girl steady her way to the floor, but they were both off-balance. They looked up at Martin with eyes that were swallowed by darkness.

"We get the best moonlight here," Martin remarked when his image was reflected in the teens' pupils.

"There's no light interference," Rowan added.

Martin's head snapped at her as if she had spoken out of turn. They stared at each other, and an old grudge threatened to bubble to the surface until Paul intervened.

"Hey, guys," he spoke nervously. "We have a job to do."

"You're right," Martin said, finally breaking his stare. "A job Morgan entrusted to *me*."

Rowan crossed her arms. She made it clear that she didn't believe in his leadership.

"Why aren't they turning?" Jessica asked.

Martin inspected Aiden. Aiden allowed him to lift his eyelids and run his finger along his gums. "Are you sure they're ready?" he barked at Rowan.

Loila started to shake. At first, it was a little tremble, but then her body almost convulsed on the floor.

"What do you have for shock?" Kaitlyn asked, bending over Loila.

I'd had enough. I was scared for Loila, but I was also mad at Aiden and Rowan. Rowan had led us to the abandoned town, knowing what was waiting for us, and Aiden had been counseled by his father to expect something like this.

"WHAT IS GOING ON?" I bellowed.

For a second, I thought I saw pity glance across Rowan's features, but then she remembered the presence of the others and she hardened her face. Martin saw her compassion, and he smirked. "Do you want to tell him?"

"Fine," Rowan huffed. "You guys act like Razz is dumb, but his father wasn't around to talk to him about it."

As Rowan spoke, I tried to map out a way to free Loila. I was pulled into her story, though, and I realized there might be a reason I could run faster, see better, and I had mysterious puffs of hair on my body.

"A couple of generations ago," she began, "a certain group of religious people were looking for ways to extend their lives. They ground up animal bones and ate them and performed rituals they made up. Of course, these people drank blood from many different animals, but someone drank the blood of an animal that changed them. He drank the blood of a werewolf."

Tears fell from my eyes at the sound of the word. Not because I believed her, but because I understood that Loila and I were on a remote hillside surrounded by crazy people.

Rowan sensed my disbelief, but she went on. "He sought out the animal that had changed him and formed a friendly alliance with him. Even though he was cautioned against it, the newly turned man understood his power and sought to share it with the world. Women were drawn to him, despite his unhygienic appearance, and he healed people."

"Tell him how," Jessica encouraged.

Rowan shot her a look of disgust, but she complied. "He wanted to try to find a way to keep himself from transforming during the full moon. He tried restraining himself, but he always broke free. He wanted more control over himself. So, he ran off to a monastery where he developed a formula from his own blood. Sometime afterward, he saw that it also took away certain sicknesses."

Martin reached into his pocket and produced a vial. The amber powder glinted off the artificial light.

"Scorn?" I said doubtfully. "But you said a couple of generations ago. This stuff has only been out since around the time we were born."

"The media is a little more skilled than they were in the early 1900's," Rowan explained. "They were busy covering wars, riots, and civil unrest."

"So, I guess you're going to tell me that the Scorn he developed caused his patients to turn into beasts," I mocked. Now that my suspicions about Rowan were confirmed, I didn't try to harness my words.

"*Patients?*" Rowan said. Her eyebrows drew together, but then she shook off my comment and returned to her explanation. "Not exactly. Small doses seemed to take away their ailments, but they kept asking him for more, even when they weren't sick. It made them feel powerful, and since most of them were peasants, they had never experienced the feeling."

"Is he the Morgan you've been talking about?"

The room erupted in laughter. The other initiates winced from the sudden sound.

"No," Martin said. "You may have to dig deep for this one," he added sarcastically. "The man Rowan was talking about was dumped in a river in the early 1900's. He was shot in the head with a silver bullet."

"Rasputin?" I questioned. "No, he was only a man."

"How many times did they try to kill him?"

I thought back. There was some historical proof that detailed the number of assassination attempts. Months before his death, he survived a stabbing, and it was possible that poison had laced the food and drinks he had been given on the night he was assassinated, but there was no irrefutable evidence that he survived multiple attempts on his life. "Are you trying to tell me that we're all descended from Rasputin?" I surmised.

"Oh, no, sweetheart," Jessica giggled. "He had his own followers. They're our parents." I mentally tried to calculate their ages if their parents had been born in the late 1800's.

"Or grandparents," Aiden chimed in. He still stared at the ground as if he were afraid to look at anyone directly.

"Aiden comes from one of the *best* families," Martin commented. Aiden looked less than proud of the distinction. Martin clapped him on the back, and he almost jumped. "He's supposedly an Elite."

"There are Bittens and Blood-Born," Rowan clarified. "You can guess what happens to make the first one, and the Blood-Bornes came from Rasputin and his followers. Elders and Elites are the wolves from the oldest bloodline."

"Didn't his dad muddy that up a bit with Savannah?" Kaitlyn said.

"Yeah," Martin agreed, "but she got what was coming to her."

At the mention of his mother, Aiden's fire ignited. In one breath his eyes became pools of blackness. He grabbed Martin by his neck and slung him against the wall. Paul rushed Aiden, pushing him into a door that hung loosely from its hinges. The door lost its hold, crashing on top of my friend.

"You still haven't mastered your strength," Paul said to Aiden, but he seemed nervous.

Jessica tried to console Martin, but he shrugged her off irritably. I noticed the golden glint in his eyes.

"Do we all have different eyes?" I asked him, trying to take Paul's attention off Aiden. I never remembered seeing a difference in Rowan's or Aiden's eyes.

"No," Paul answered. "That's only the elder bloodline."

"Are you an elder?" I directed at Rowan.

"No."

"Her, an elder?" Kelly guffawed. "She was a half-eaten meal."

Suddenly, it all made sense to me, but if I admitted that it was true then I'd have to question my own sanity. I decided to buy Loila more time by relating my understanding.

"You're the cheerleader they found fifteen years ago in Lost Cove," I said to Rowan. "But I thought you died?"

"I thought I died, too," Rowan said. "One of the initiates tore into me." She brushed the scar on her arm and shoulder. "But he didn't finish the job."

"Coward," Martin growled.

"Yeah," Rowan sighed. "Why would he have shown any compassion to an unarmed girl?"

"It was his task to eat you," Martin barked.

"He was my boyfriend!" Rowan yelled back. "He wanted to let me go, but you two wouldn't let him do it." She directed her accusations at Martin and Kelly, and I fit that part of the story together. They were the same cheer captain and brother from years ago. But how was it possible? Rowan, Martin, and Kelly still looked like teenagers. *How many unsuspecting teenage girls had they lured to their deaths?*

"Guys!" Kelly yelled. "Give it a rest! Rowan's one of us, so we don't need to fight over the reason for it."

Loila was starting to stir, so I asked another question to give her time to wake up. "Why didn't anyone recognize you?"

"They did," Rowan said, and suddenly I knew.

"Mrs. Holt is your sister." I shook my head in disbelief. "You fight like you know each other, and you said that your sister wanted you to help with the decorations."

Rowan put her finger on the end of her nose to indicate that I was right. "She's the one who found me here."

I was the only one in the room who was shocked by the connection. Even Aiden, who had dusted himself off from his clash with Paul, didn't seem surprised.

"I was dragged back here to die on my own," Rowan continued, "but my sister never gave up hope that she'd find me. Luckily, she wasn't alone. There used to be a man who lived up here," she held up her arm again, "with an injury that looked a lot like mine. He cared for me until the next full moon. After that, everything healed, but I still had the scar."

I thought I saw Jessica smirk. Rowan was a natural beauty, and Jessica seemed to believe that the scar detracted from her image, but the rest of Rowan's coffee-colored skin was flawless.

Martin was standing closest to the door, so his expression was the first to change. One by one, our captors lost their color and bowed their heads. My heart did a double beat and skipped, as the room seemed to suck in its breath. What could have caused the monsters who took Loila to react with that much fear?

CHAPTER THIRTY-THREE

A woman with long, dark hair and deep brown eyes stepped into the house, cataloging the number of submissive teens.

Monique! I thought, but I corrected myself. The woman was a cold shadow of my mom's best friend. She snarled in disgust at the state of the dilapidated dwelling.

"Morgan," Martin said.

"I thought I would walk into a feeding," she replied. "Is this a ladies' sewing circle?"

No one spoke.

"Huh?" she continued. "Well, I can only conclude that you have decided to make friends with your food."

"No, ma'am," Paul piped up. "We were just waiting on her to wake up."

Morgan stared down at Loila, who was now fully awake. "Do I have to tell you how to begin?" she said condescendingly.

I couldn't take my eyes off of the woman who looked so much like someone with whom I had shared meals, love, and laughter. They even moved the same, but Morgan didn't have Monique's limp. She noticed my open-mouthed stare and smirked.

"You thought I was my sister," she mocked. "Did you think I was here to save you from the mean old monsters?"

Martin chuckled. I attempted to seem apathetic.

"You can pretend like all this" —she gestured around the room— "doesn't bother you, but we both know the truth." She forced herself to laugh, and the sound made me more uncomfortable. Crossing the room and lifting Loila by the back of her dress, she told me, "That's why I chose this one. You need to see her ripped apart, if you don't do it yourself. That's the only way you can accept who you really are."

"Why can't we just drink pig's blood, or something?" Aiden squeaked. He was taking a big chance by speaking up, but he didn't want Loila hurt either.

"Pig's blood?" she laughed. When no one joined her, she glared at the other teenagers and they added their coerced amusement. "Have you ever tasted pig's blood?"

She crossed the room until she towered over Aiden. His head was still down, shoulders slumped. "You're Bradley's cub, aren't you?" Aiden nodded a little too fast, and Morgan smiled at his nervousness. "Your blood is tainted with the emotions of your human mother," she spat. "Look at you." She pretended to survey him physically. "You can't even stand tall in the presence of a blood-born Lycan."

Blood-born? I thought. *Did that mean that Monique was a werewolf too?*

I thought back on the years I had known her. She had some rough patches, but my mom had insisted it was because of her past drug problems. Then I remembered the last month when I had thought she had taken the contents of the vial she had swiped from under my mattress. She hadn't sampled it, but she was run-down for a week, and my mom had cited feminine issues. *Had I just been willfully blind?*

No, I decided. I had absolutely no reason to believe that my mom's best friend was a werewolf.

Morgan was all business. Martin handed her a powder that she sprinkled on Loila like salt. "When I let this girl go, you will run after her. Whoever catches her will have an uninterrupted meal until he or she allows the rest to join him or her. That person will lead this small pack."

I vowed that I would stay still. I hoped that Aiden and the others would follow my example. If they didn't, then I would fight them. I would tear each of them or all of them apart until Loila was safe.

The smell of the sprinkled powder reached my nose, and my body ran away from my mind. My physical senses overtook my emotions, and all that was left was a dull, throbbing hunger. It was a hunger I couldn't define, but it pressed on me like the weight of a vicious animal with a voracious appetite.

Loila saw the change in the kids around her and she struggled. "You won't make it far," Morgan ridiculed. She let her go.

Even though she had been struggling to get away, Loila locked eyes with me and remained motionless. She had adopted my plan without the knowledge of it.

I forced myself to think thoughts of our trips to the cave, our inside jokes, or anything that would keep my mind sane. Loila kept fazing out, a blurry image that I tried to focus on. I thought I was going to lose my fight against myself.

My body only changed a little. Instead of turning into a full werewolf, my hair puffed in sporadic pockets on my arms and face and my vision shifted. I could see things more crisply, almost smelling my sight.

My nose tingled with the electric, metallic scent of blood, and it was too much to ignore. Loila's face constricted in terror, but I didn't care. I was hungry, and she wasn't one of us, so she was food.

Four werewolves lunged at Loila, but Morgan knocked us back with a wave of her hand. We bent our heads, stricken.

"The meal is nothing without the chase," she barked. She dragged Loila to the door. "Run, girl!"

Loila pushed herself away from the doorframe as if she wanted to sprint, but she stopped. Saliva was trickling out of my mouth, and all I could smell was her flowery perfume and her syrupy sweet blood.

I caught a glimpse of Aiden. He had turned, his body lean and elongated, with full gray fur. He held his arms up timidly, as though he was pushing himself back.

The six other kids remained human. They had called themselves werewolves, but they didn't seem to be experiencing the same physical changes or mental conflicts.

I should be resisting, I thought. *Loila is my friend.*

I couldn't master my body with my mind, so I made physical moves to prevent myself from attacking her. I pushed myself into the wall, and I held my breath.

"How cute," Morgan laughed. "You don't want to eat your friend. Well, there are three other beasties here who will devour her and one of them will lead your pack!"

Morgan let go of Loila and pushed her, but Loila stood firmly in the doorway. I begged her to go, because I knew that I would consume her if I had to breathe in her smell again. She was beautiful. She was radiant. She was filled with blood.

Loila tried to have faith in Aiden and me. I could sense her distress, but I could also feel her friendship. Years of summer swims and secret late-night calls were sent to me in a glance. I took a small, pre-emptive breath. I almost lost myself again in the aroma of blood, jasmine, and sweat, but I managed to keep calm and stand.

The boy and girl that Jessica and Kaitlyn had brought were lining Loila in their view. Any moment, they would pounce on her.

"Stop!" I commanded. My voice sound thick and garbled to me, but it had a resounding effect on the other three werewolf pups in the room. At first, the boy I didn't know eyed me, willing me to look away, but his head finally dropped in defeat.

"Stupid girl!" Morgan yelled, grabbing Loila's dress and throwing her back onto the floor. "I said it was time to eat, pups!"

Three sets of eyes flicked to me. In that moment, I became their alpha.

"No," I answered resolutely.

Morgan took two long strides and slapped me. My body flew across the room, landing on Jessica. She whimpered from her injuries. I tried to help her when I rose, but she shoved my hand away. "I don't need help for a weak little pup."

"Eat your meal!" Morgan demanded the others, pointing to Loila, who was shivering again.

I had to force the words out of my mouth, but I pushed through my strong animal urges to say, "Never!"

The girl in my new pack whined, but she made no move to go against me. The boy put his furry arm over her to try to shield her from her hunger.

"You are blithering idiots!" Morgan shouted at us. "This is how you learn. This is how you eat. This is how you satisfy the raw, nagging hunger that overpowers you every time the moon is full." She shook her fist at us. "Do you know how many times I have denied my hunger?" She stared at us with wide, brown eyes. "I refused myself a taste of my friend too, but he was eaten anyway, and I had to wait until my sister defected before I could assume the role that was meant for me."

Memories of my talks about drugs with Monique floated back to me. Was she really talking about drugs, or had she been trying to tell me about the urges that consumed her every time a full moon was at its zenith?

"EAT!" Morgan thundered, but it had little impact on the werewolves in my pack now that I was their leader.

"Enough!"

We all directed our attention at the sound of the voice, and a hooded figure entered the room. His robe hung on him loosely, spilling waves of material across his midsection and legs. It swayed when he walked, reminding me of ocean waves in the dark.

Morgan opened her mouth to speak, but he shushed her by placing one finger to his lips. "The acolytes are here?" he questioned.

Morgan nodded and lowered her eyes.

"Then let them take care of the girl," he instructed. "The objective was to find the alpha in the pack, and it is now clear who that is."

I didn't like the inference he made about Loila. I had a strong pull to keep my head down, but I physically fought against it to lift my head.

"I am taking her off this mountain," I asserted.

The hooded figure responded to me indirectly. "He can take her off this hill, but she will not be breathing."

"My father can have her memory wiped," Aiden voiced, and fell to the floor. It had taken all his strength to speak in the presence of a greater alpha than the other pack leaders in the room.

"Hypnosis is a useful tool," the hooded figure agreed. He crossed the room and crouched in front of Loila. He touched her cheek tenderly and pinch it. Loila flinched at the pain, and I took a step forward. I was blocked from moving closer by something I could only feel. It was like an invisible forcefield was blocking contact.

"Loila." He spoke as if he were speaking to his own child. Loila was drawn to the sound of her name, and he held her gaze. "You were at the dance," he continued in an intimate lilt. Loila nodded, and he picked up her hand. "You danced with Rasputin, and you drank the punch. Someone poured alcohol in the punch, and you felt ill. You stumbled in the street, but your friends helped you."

Loila nodded dreamily, fully entranced by his hypnotic suggestions. "I have good friends," she responded in a daze.

"Yes," he spoke softly. "Now rest until you are back home."

Loila collapsed on the floor in a heap. The man placed her hand over her stomach and rose.

My breath had caught while he spoke to Loila. He had called me "Rasputin," and aside from people who didn't know me, or teachers at the beginning of the school year, only one other person had called me by my full first name.

CHAPTER THIRTY-FOUR

"Dad?"

The man lifted his hood and faced me fully. He was my father, and he had hardly changed. The golden flecks in his blue-green eyes stood out more and he didn't hold himself with the same posture, but he beckoned me with strong arms. I rushed to him, grateful that he was alive.

"How?" I asked after a short embrace. I couldn't stop looking at him. I didn't want to take my eyes off him and lose him again.

"How did you expect him to do any work with *you* hanging around?" Morgan spat at me. "You were always trying to find him and bring him back to your human mother."

My dad shot her a look, and she bowed her head, but only marginally. "You know I'm right, Grigori," she forced.

"But the bear—"

My father stopped me. "It wasn't a bear," he explained. "Another wolf" —he paused, searching for the right word— "*disagreed* with me, and we tumbled through the woods. Afterward, it seemed like a good idea to make you believe I was dead."

"But why?" I could feel tears welling up in my eyes, and I hated myself for letting my emotions show. My hurt was unwelcome in a room full of people who didn't deserve to see me in that condition anyway.

"I was in a bad place," he revealed. "I was in constant danger, and I couldn't get back to you, your sister, and your mom until my work was finished. I mean, look what happened to me in the woods. The other werewolf could have attacked you." He put his hand on my shoulder. "Everything I did was to protect you."

I wanted to argue that I would have kept his secret. I wanted to say that my family was worse off because of his ruse. But I could only stand there with hurt over time lost. The fur on my body receded, almost like drumming fingers tickling across my skin. It wasn't unlike the feeling I had when I feel asleep on my arm, and I woke to the tingling of blood returning to my appendage.

Aiden and the other initiates had almost returned to normal. Their pupils still covered their eyes, but their bodies and actions were much more human.

My father introduced the two other kids as Bruce and Danielle. Danielle liked to be called Danni. They went to a public school in a nearby county, and they were both on the track team.

"They're the best in their division," my father chuckled, when they spoke about their speed and agility. I mentioned to him how quickly Rowan, Aiden, and I had run to Lost Cove.

"Didn't you wonder why it only took you an hour to run so far without the need to stop?" he asked.

I thought about Aiden's brief water break, but I didn't mention it. Martin had already attacked his lineage because of his mother.

I made an effort to get to know Danni and Bruce, but I didn't bond with them. Morgan watched my interactions like a trained bird and offered her perspective. "It's all about the hunt," she explained. "You remember the feeling of running through the woods with your pack. It's how you learn to communicate." She threw up her hands at us. "You can't learn to lead a pack by having a playdate with your daddy watching!"

"That's enough," my father barked, and Morgan whelped. "I remember your parents standing behind you."

There were so many things I wanted to say to my father, but we were around strangers. Finally, Morgan, the matriarch of her den, gathered at the door with Kelly, Martin, Paul, Kaitlyn, and Jessica. Aiden locked eyes with me, and I realized that he was asking permission to leave with Danni and Bruce. I nodded my assent.

"Tell my sister I'm sorry," Rowan whispered.

"Can't you talk to her at school on Monday?"

Rowan smiled at my naiveite. "I was placed in your school because I still look like a teenager, and because I needed to guide you up here for the Ritual."

Part of me had already known that Rowan wasn't going back to school. I had sensed her differentness on the first day she was there, but now that I knew her, I didn't want her to go.

"Stephanie and I had a deal," Rowan went on. "I told her that I had never gotten to experience the things she had, like dances and having real friends, so she said I could stick around until the banquet."

"Doesn't she want to see you every day?" I asked, sneaking a look at my father while he awkwardly bid farewell to Morgan. "She almost lost you."

Rowan understood the duplicity of my question. "She doesn't want me to be noticed," she clarified. "If people learn about us" —she motioned to our group— "they'll kill us and dissect us. Not to mention the wild packs that would be hunted down."

I realized that I had only glanced the surface of a much larger set of beings that had survived for countless generations. They relied on myths and secrecy to keep them safe.

"I'll tell her," I promised, and then I asked, "Isn't your name really Mae?"

"I changed it," she said, looking down for the first time since I'd met her. "There could have been people in the town who might have remembered me if they'd heard my old name. I like the name, though. I'm going to keep it."

"Rowan."

Rowan responded immediately to Morgan by turning, but I grabbed her arm. "You stay with *her*?"

Rowan laughed. "Morgan took me in. She didn't have to accept me—since I was bitten and not blood-borne—but I run with her son's pack."

I couldn't hide my surprise. "Martin's her son."

"Good job," Rowan remarked in a patronizing tone. "I'm sure you'll figure out a lot more if you think about it." She let her cryptic words hang in the air.

Rowan obediently followed her den mother. The pack trickled out into the night, and my father and I were left alone, with Loila unconscious between us.

"Was she your date?' my father asked.

"No," I told him quickly. I thought about the lengths I had gone to protect her, and I quickly added, "But I like her."

It didn't improve the awkwardness between my father and me, and both of us searched for another subject. Finally, my father threw Loila over his shoulder and motioned for me to follow him.

"What about the light?"

"Beaux will get it," he said.

I didn't ask more about the vague reference to another person. I assumed it was one of the acolytes he had mentioned to Morgan. I wondered if they were waiting somewhere nearby, hoping to be called upon by one of the beasts they worshiped.

The sky was a deep sea of darkness and the trees swallowed us in the abyss. I would have been completely lost if it wouldn't have been for my acute vision and hearing. I instinctively navigated the landscape, sidestepping trees and managing the terrain.

"How many times have I been here?" I asked my father.

"We used to hike these mountains all the time with Hannah. She and her husband came up here with you, your mom, and me."

"She gave me peppermints," I commented. I took one out of my pants pocket and handed it to him. I popped the other mint into my mouth. Hannah may have wanted me to savor the dance in the memories I associated with the peppermints, but I thought when I was on a hike with my long-lost father was a much better time to have them.

"I guess this means that we'll always remember our experience," my father chuckled. "On the night of your eighth-grade dance, I carried your little girlfriend down the mountain after she was almost eaten in a Lycan ritual."

He was making polite conversation, but his casual attitude hurt me. *Hadn't he missed me? Didn't he want to explain the reason he had left?*

I decided to remain silent and wait for him to speak. I was tired of trying to please him when he had abandoned me with a lame excuse that it was in my best interest.

The silence was comfortable at first, but after a while it swelled to cover the entire mountain. We emerged from the forest, bathed in moonlight, and aligned ourselves with the tracks that led back to town. My father knew that I purposely wasn't speaking, but the silence remained unbroken.

We picked up the vibrations of a train as it raced down the mountain. Our senses were heightened, and we had plenty of time to move off the track before the train rushed past us. I wondered how hard it would have been for a regular person to have gotten off the tracks in time.

The number of cars on the train passed more quickly than they did in town. We resumed our trek while the large gravel between the trestles shifted under our feet.

I almost asked a number of questions, but I stopped before they passed my lips. I was determined to make my father talk to me. Finally, after an eternity of missed opportunities, he spoke.

"You're mad at me."

It wasn't a question, so I kept quiet. I hoped he would continue, taking whatever he wanted from my silence.

He sighed. "My father wasn't much better, and I hated him, so you must not be buying my reasons for leaving."

I didn't commit my feelings to my voice. I let the gravel sing under my feet as I picked up my pace. My father easily matched my steps, even with Loila's extra weight. I worried about her head hanging limply down my father's back and then I decided that she was doing much better than when she first arrived in Lost Cove.

"I was an illegitimate son," my father said abruptly. Maybe he was nervous, too, and he was looking for a natural beginning to his story.

We had talked about the present and the past, but I had the feeling that we should be discussing something in the middle. I let him continue his diatribe, in hopes that it would bring us to the answers for my questions.

"We moved to this country before I could remember our village, but my mom talked about it all the time. My father died when I was young, so I didn't have anyone to tell me about the changes that started when I was your age."

"Did you have a random ball of hair?" I asked.

He laughed. "Yeah, it was on my calf. I was certain everyone could see it when I walked."

"Mine was under one of my arms and I shaved it," I confessed.

We chuckled, but our smiles fell quickly, and my father resumed his narrative. "I thought that I was going crazy. I could see things in bright light, and I heard voices calling me at night. When my cycles started, I could feel the change coming on me, and I ran into the woods. It's almost like I knew that I had to get away from my mother and my brother."

It was the first time my father had talked about his brother. I racked my mind, and I couldn't remember hearing anything about any of his family.

"When I turned into a full werewolf, I was drawn to my pack. I could feel them the way you can sense that someone is in the room with you, even when your back is turned. We tracked the scent of a deer and overcame it easily. We shared the meat and turned back when the sun came up."

He seemed to reflect on the memory. "I guess Morgan is right about that," he conceded. "Tracking and eating with your pack brings you together."

"Do you hunt humans?" I interjected.

My father missed a step and almost fell. He balanced Loila on his shoulder and resumed walking at a faster pace. An old injury awakened, and he betrayed a limp. It was a small difference, but it reminded me of something.

"I don't agree with hunting humans," he answered.

I noticed that his language was precise. He didn't truly answer my question.

"It wasn't easy living in a small town after I started turning," he went on. "Even though my pack was nearby, I didn't really fit in with the locals. My mom had a Slavic accent, and it took her a long time to learn English. A lot of people believed she was crazy, so they thought I was just like her.

"I took my pack into the mountains, and we looked for places to hide away from the—"

"Who was in your pack?" I cut in.

My father lifted his head and appeared thoughtful. "Well, there was Jeffery," he recalled. "He was the smartest, and he was good at chemistry. Then Mary, she was the best tracker out of all of us. William read every book he could find, and Bethie, his sister, was the sweetest little girl, but she was the first to put her teeth on a kill if I told her that she could do it. And Hannah," he finished. "She was the most ambitious out of us, but I guess you know that. She's had a thriving business."

"Something he said had struck me. "You sound like you've lived forever."

"It feels like it," he sighed. "I have lived a good, long while."

"How long?"

He quickly changed the subject. "How was Hannah?"

I wasn't going to let him placate me with half-truths vague answers. I decided to steer the conversation where it really needed to go. "She was fine, and I'm sure you know that. Why did you leave your family?"

The question hung in the air between us. Finally, he spoke. "Rasputin, there are so many things you don't understand."

"Try me."

"I had secrets."

"Yeah, I know," I replied sarcastically. "But Aiden's father is a piece of crap, and he still took the time to tell Aiden what was happening to him. He didn't just peace out when things got too hard."

"I didn't 'peace out,'" my father said, and a note of irritation edged his words. "I left the house to keep my family out of danger, and when you kept following me around, I knew that my death would be the only thing that would keep you away from me."

"What was so important then?" I pleaded. "And why didn't you come back when it was over?"

My father sighed and rubbed his temples with the inside of his thumb and forefinger. "It will never be over," he breathed.

"Why?"

"Because there's always someone looking for an artificial high!" he shouted.

Loila moaned in her sleep, and my father repositioned her. I had another question on my lips when my father spoke again.

"It's hard to turn," my father said. "Healthy werewolves that obey the natural laws can live a long time, but every exposure to a full moon depletes us immeasurably. Over the month, we build back up, but then the end of the cycle drains us. I won't even tell you what a blue moon, super moon, or lunar eclipse can do."

"Sounds like I have a lot to look forward to," I commented.

"That's what concerned Jeffery, too," my father said, without acknowledging my sarcasm. "He poured though biochemistry books, and even made it through pre-medicine courses in college, before he found a way to suppress our urges."

The puzzle pieces were fitting together for me, but I didn't like the picture. "Jeffery made Scorn, didn't he?"

"Yes," my father replied, visibly grateful that I understood most of the situation. "But we called it Moon's Bane. Jeffery made a couple of experimental doses that were okay, and they kept our urges to hunt down, but the last formula he developed kept us fully human during the full moon."

"So, when a werewolf takes Scorn, it keeps them from turning into a werewolf?" I asked.

"Yeah," he responded. "Jeffery made it from his own blood, so he manipulated it to keep a werewolf from reacting to the moon." My father chuckled. "He used to call it his allergy shot, since we all have a reaction to the moon."

"Shouldn't the people who take Scorn turn into werewolves? I mean, Rowan was bitten, and she turned into a werewolf."

"That's a logical assumption," he agreed, "but actually, the blood used for the experiment was taken when Jeffery was not in werewolf form, so I guess it just makes humans go crazy and get a little aggressive."

I thought about the look of terror on Tabitha's face and what she had experienced with her parents. "It makes them act like werewolves without turning. They have the hunger for blood."

"The government has done a pretty good job of carting off the ones that got out of hand," my father said spitefully.

"Have they found a way to turn them back?"

"No, buddy," he spoke. "I think they still have them in those cages in New Mexico. Well, at least the ones who have survived their experiments."

My anger had been mounting, and it erupted like a volcano. "So, werewolves just ruin lives!" I yelled. A nocturnal creature screamed its disapproval over my outburst. "They leave their kids, let their blood pollute the good parents, and fake their own deaths!"

My father let Loila slide down his arm and land on the ground. She fell into a comfortable heap.

"I've had enough," he said. His voice stayed at a regular volume, but I understood that I had crossed a line. "Little boy, you have a lot to learn.

"First of all, Jeffery never meant for his formula to be taken by humans. The people in our pack tested it, and we gave it to a few other packs when it worked. When news spread about it, we had orders from all over the world. Aiden's father helped us distribute them, but somewhere along the way, Savannah picked up a vial and became an addict."

"Aiden's mom was the first human to take it?" I gasped.

My father reshouldered Loila, and we continued our trek. The sky was so dark that it commanded the earth around us to be still, holding its breath for sunrise.

"We think so, but we can't be sure," he answered. "She was the first human close to us who had taken it, but we had been using Moon's Bane for years before Bradley married her. Anyway, by the time Savannah was killed, there were vials of Jeffery's serum floating around everywhere. Lycans were told to be careful, but I don't know how many of them listened to us."

I stared at my father, really noticing the injury that had slowed him down. "You were at the factory, weren't you?"

He nodded. "I believed you were there because you had started to turn, so I tossed you a vial to keep you from turning during your next cycle. I thought you already knew what was going on."

"Well, I didn't," I pouted.

"I know that now," he said, "but only after I sent Beaux to find you."

I remembered my odd encounter with Beaux at the convenience store. "You could have told him to be less creepy about it."

"He couldn't just come out and tell you to come see me. Everyone thinks I'm dead, so he had to be cryptic."

Loila moaned in her sleep, and I was reminded about the horror she had experienced. "And what about the Rituals?" I asked. "Why do you let them happen?"

"I don't," he responded. "I kept Morgan from going through those practices since Rowan was bitten. She thought she could cause you to turn faster if she had a Ritual. I think she was right."

"But why did she choose Loila?"

My father readjusted my friend. Her dress created a ripple of light. "Some Lycans have turned as early as nine years old when they don't have other friends," he revealed. "They are more attune to their pack during the full moon. I guess she thought you would assume your role sooner without your friend."

I was grateful for his straight-forward answer, but I wasn't finished with my machine gun questioning. "Why don't you run with your pack anymore? Do they all think you're dead?"

"No, they know that I'm alive," he said. "The ones that are living, anyway."

"What does that mean?"

"That's what I've been trying to tell you. It's dangerous. I've already lost so many of my friends."

I stayed quiet while he reflected. Hopefully, my silence would give me more answers.

"William and Bethie were the first ones," he began, and I thought I heard his voice crack. "They caught them in the woods and shot them."

"Bullets can kill werewolves, can they?"

"They can if they're made of silver," he replied.

I wonder something I didn't ask. *If William and Bethie were killed with silver bullets, then did 'they' know the siblings were werewolves?*

"Then Mary and I met after their funeral, and we were backed into an alley. I was able to jump the wall, but Mary—"

He didn't have to finish.

"Jeffery thought he was safe. He held a pretty prestigious position at a government facility. One day, though, he was rushed out of his lab by the guards, or what he thought were the guards. In the middle of the day, they drove him off in a black SUV. I tracked him until I found a lab coat covered in his blood. There were bullet holes in it, and there were no other signs of him.

"After that, I broke into his house and the houses of people who knew him. I guess you remember that," he said to me.

I gave a noncommitted grunt.

"Now, you're old enough to know that I was looking for his notebook. He was the one who made Moon's Bane, or Scorn, and Bradley, Hannah, and I still needed it. Buyers were begging Bradley for more of the product, but we didn't know how to make it."

"Did you find it?"

"I think whoever took Jeffery took the notebook, too," my father sighed. "Hannah and I found some of his old notes in the glovebox of the rusted, old truck up in Lost Cove, so we could make more Moon's Bane, but Jeffery had told us that he had developed something new. It was a formula that could transfer years of a person's life to another person."

"That's pretty neat," I commented.

"I'm not going to get into the ideology of it with you," my father said gravely, "but there are so many negative applications to that process."

I thought about corporeal punishment and my situation at home. "Maybe they could give cancer patients the years of the murderers and rapists."

My father took a deep breath. "Like I said, I'm not going to debate the philosophy of his claim with you, but I understand why you say that. How is your mom?"

I felt like he'd thrown ice water over me. Part of me wanted to tell him everything and beg for his help, but the other part of me wanted to remain guarded and keep news about my family away from him. After all, he had left us. Why did he deserve to know anything?

"You already know, so why are you asking me?"

The words were already out of my mouth before I thought about them. They were true, though, and he didn't deny it.

"I love her," he said simply. "It will be hard to see her go."

"Why don't you save her then?" I demanded. "You have a way to keep her alive, but you'd rather have her believe that you're dead."

My father turned on me quickly and grabbed my collar. He lifted me a couple of inches off the ground with one hand before he realized what he was doing and let me down, hardly moving the gravel under my feet.

"Don't you know anything?" he yelled. "Sure, I could give your mom the Scorn from the factory, but it would only make her better for a couple of months. Then she'd have to have another dose, and another dose."

He jabbed my shoulder with the tips of his fingers. "It's not a cure!" he shouted. "How many beasts does the government put in cages and execute at the end of their cycle?"

"They execute them?" The air was so soundless that it felt like the forest around us was listening.

My father grunted in my direction. "Then they dissect them. They used to claim that they were trying to find a way to cure them, but really they just want to weaponize them."

"They dissect them," I repeated.

"Otherwise, their containment facility would be overrun in a month."

"How do *you* know?" I accused.

"I've been there. I rescued" —he paused— "*someone*, and I saw the inner workings of the facility."

"Why don't you stop it?" I demanded. "You and your friends are these big, powerful Lycans that spread fear and eat little girls" —I motioned to Loila— "but you can't storm in that facility when the moon is full?"

"How much control did you have when you turned?" my father questioned.

"Enough to know that I shouldn't eat my friend," I quipped.

"All *my* friends are Lycan," my father laughed.

"You didn't eat my mom," I said.

He grew quiet, and the wind whipped through our hair. "No, son," he spoke. "I never hurt your mom. I was always far away whenever I changed, and I used quite a bit of Moon's Bane to stay with her."

"Do you even care?" I spat. "She's going to die. Maybe she thinks that she'll see her husband when she dies, and you won't be there for her then either!"

"I wouldn't have been there anyway," he responded gruffly. "When you're dead, that's it. Game over."

I could feel my anger bubbling to the surface. I kept trying to push it back down, but it frothed and rose until it spilled over.

I didn't like it, but I could recognize the selfishness within my father's pack. I understood his need to fake his own death. However, I didn't know why he had to let my mom suffer and die.

"I hate you," I told him. "I want you to get us back to town, and I never want to see you again."

My father fumbled through a strained apology, stiffened up, and stopped talking. We walked the last several miles in silence.

The sky turned lighter hues of blue over the mountains to the east. I thought about my mom, and I wondered how worried she, Monique, and Lexi were about me. My mom had probably called the police to report me as a missing teenager.

Mrs. Holt was waiting faithfully at her vehicle. She opened the car door and scanned the area for Rowan.

"She left with Morgan," I informed her.

A look moved across her face, but she quickly reshuffled her emotions. She nodded at Loila. "I'm glad that were able to save her. I like her."

She flashed her keys. "I guess the two of you will need a ride back to town."

It took me a moment to realize she was leaving out my dad. Mrs. Holt understood more than me. She had left her sister in the forest. She knew my father couldn't go back with me.

"I guess I'll see you in another six years," I scoffed.

"Or when you need me to help you rescue another one of your little girlfriends," he returned.

I climbed into Mrs. Holt's backseat and my father laid Loila carefully over me. I cradled her head in my hand.

"Snap your fingers and say 'lock picker' when you want her to wake up," he told me.

I wasn't softened by the memory the phrase pulled up. I was convinced that my father was a horrible person, or beast, and I wasn't going to let him forget it.

"Be careful," he said seriously. "I love you, Rasputin."

I squirmed in my seat, wishing his eyes were anywhere but on me.

"Don't get eaten by a bear," I shot back.

My father thanked Mrs. Holt and walked to the back of the vehicle. I could feel him watching us as we pulled away, but I didn't look back.

CHAPTER THIRTY-FIVE

I walked into my door without fanfare. My mom was drinking orange juice and Monique held a mug of coffee in her hand.

"How was the sleepover at Aiden's?" Monique asked casually.

I was dumbfounded. Who had planted the lie that saved me from facing my mom? I was almost ready to wave dismissively and slink to my room when my mom screeched, "What did you do to your suit?"

She tried to jump up from her chair, but dizziness knocked her back. She concentrated on a spot on the wall for a moment, and rose slowly, without the same vigor that she'd had when she'd noticed the condition of my clothes.

"How can I bring this suit back to Hannah?"

"I'll do it," Monique volunteered, sipping her coffee without looking up.

"It's only right for me to do it," my mom said resolutely, surveying the stains and tears on the slacks.

"Is this a wine stain?" my mom asked about a blood splatter.

I was unsure about how it got there, but I had a lie prepared. "Aiden found some blueberries."

"He ate random berries?"

"It's *Aiden*," Monique said as if it explained everything.

"You knew it was important to me to return this suit in a good condition," my mom sighed. "This is so unlike you." I stared back at her with stoicism, hoping that she wouldn't dismantle whatever lie had been constructed.

"He's fourteen," Monique piped up. "He rough housed with one of his friends. They rolled down a few hills, probably stayed out later than they were supposed to, and ate a few berries that could have killed them." She glanced up at my mom and me and winked, "Does that sound about right?"

"Yeah," I said, rolling my lie around in my mouth before I said it. "Aiden pushed me down a hill. It's no big deal."

My mom's eyebrows shot up. "It may be no big deal to Aiden's father if Aiden messes up his suit, but your suit was rented."

"And it was rented from a real—"

"Monique!" my mom cut in quickly. "Hannah is just a strict businesswoman."

"Who was infatuated with your husband, so she treats you like" —a quick look from my mom changed Monique's language— "dirt," she finished.

My mom softened, and tears threatened to spill from her eyes. "Did you have a good time at the banquet?"

A sharp pain reminded me that it was the last big event my mom would share with me. I felt guilty that I had ruined the experience for her. She should have been able to pick me up and hear about the dancing, music, and awkward conversations. It seemed like she had been robbed of another normal expectation.

"It was fine, Mom," I replied, keeping my voice steady.

"Did you dance with anyone?"

"We made a line and danced around the room," I told her. "Aiden tipped the DJ to play the 'Chicken Dance' until one of the teachers made the DJ stop."

"That was Mrs. Hughes," my mom informed me. "She called me when you and Aiden ran off with that girl."

I was still unsure of how much my mom knew about my evening, and I fumbled for a half-truth. Monique saved me again.

"We were lucky Mrs. Holt took care of it," she said. "I heard that they expelled Rowan for leaving the dance, though."

For a heartbeat, I worried that Aiden and I were expelled too, but then she added, "It was really nice of you boys to try to help her. Some people can't be saved."

I could piece together the lie Mrs. Holt had told my mom with Monique's help. She had made Rowan into a troubled teen who I had tried to save. Of course, Aiden and I wouldn't be punished. We were only trying to help.

I backed into the hallway.

"Are you going to take a shower?" my mom called after me.

I nodded.

"Put what's left of your suit on a hanger and I'll take it to Hannah tomorrow." She hung her head on the way back to her chair. Monique shot up and helped her into her seat.

I peeled off my suit and put it on a wire hanger that angled off the towel rack. I was left alone with my thoughts in the shower.

Mrs. Holt had been great. Not only had she covered for me during the time I was in Lost Cove, but she had talked to Loila's parents, too. I had waited in her car while she stood at the door with the police. She blamed Loila's soiled appearance and disappearance on Rowan. I snapped my fingers and spoke the words to wake up Loila before the police came to the car, slipping the emerald ring onto her right ring finger. I hoped she'd be wearing it the next time I saw her. Loila's parents and the police stared at me like I was a criminal until Mrs. Holt told them that I had untied Loila's hands and carried her down the mountain.

Her mother threw her arms around me and cried. Her father asked me if I would take a reward. I refused the reward and transferred her mother from my shoulder to her father's chest.

Loila looked blankly into space. Occasionally, she would blink, and I'd think she was fully awake, but then she'd settle into a faraway stare again. Mrs. Holt told Loila's parents that they'd need to take her to the hospital.

Loila's parents encouraged her to thank me. She repeated the words, in a soft, willowy voice. I was on her last porch step when she added, "She tried to warn me."

"Who?" I asked her. Everyone held a collective breath.

"She sent a text. She said my friends were monsters."

When Loila spoke of monsters, she was easily dismissed by her parents and the police. Mrs. Holt and I knew the truth behind her words.

"Will Loila remember anything at all?" I asked when Mrs. Holt turned down the road to my house.

"No," she answered. "No one remembers anything a werewolf wants them to forget."

I was glad that Loila wouldn't remember the black eyes and hungry teeth that barred at her. Part of me was happy that she wouldn't see me as otherworldly, but another part of me wished that I could sit in our cave and talk about my new abilities. She would have had a fresh perspective on the things my father had told me.

I thought back to the day I had kissed her in Monique's classroom. *Why had it been so important for Loila to read the texts sent to her before the end of the day? Who had texted her?* I thought of Rowan, but it didn't quite fit.

Rowan had been more concerned with me than with Loila, and she had done nothing to try to save her from the Ritual.

After my shower, I fell onto my bed. I was almost asleep when a soft tapping woke me.

"Go away, Lexi," I huffed.

The door opened. I was about to throw my pillow full force at my sister until I saw Monique standing over me. She unceremoniously sat on my bed.

We stared at each other for a long time, each of us willing the other person to speak so we would know where to begin. Finally, I found a way to move the conversation along without giving in.

"Well, I'm going to go to sleep now," I told her, and made a show of fluffing my pillow.

"Are you okay?"

Her question caught me off guard. "Yeah," I responded automatically.

She nodded and bit her lip, bringing color to her mouth.

"How was my sister?"

"She was" —I searched for the right words— "not like you."

"Yeah," Monique chuckled. "I could describe her, but your mom wouldn't like my language."

She picked up one of my comic books and threw it at me. A werewolf screamed across the cover.

"It's like part of you always knew," she remarked.

I smiled. "I don't think so."

"We all go through denial," Monique said. "You try to tell everyone that your eyes are hazel when they change and that ball of hair on your back is a surge of teenage hormones."

"It was harder for me to explain why I could see better without my glasses."

"I bet it was!" Monique conceded. "I didn't have glasses, so I didn't have to worry about that part."

"I thought your parents were werewolves, though," I remarked.

"So, you did see your father," Monique concluded. "He's the only person who'll mention them in front of my sister."

"Are you a—"

"Werewolf?" Monique said before me. "Yes."

I flicked some dirt from under my nail. "Did you know what was happening to me?"

"Yes," she replied simply. "I knew from the first golden glint I saw in your eye."

"Why didn't you tell me?"

"How would I have started that conversation?" she asked me. "I could have told you, but would you have believed me? I had finally decided to talk to you about it, but my sister stepped in."

"Aiden's father told him," I sulked. "He was more prepared than me."

"Yeah, Aiden's *father*," she emphasized. "As much as I wish I was, I am not part of your family."

I thought back to my feelings about Monique the day before, and I shook my head. "You've been here for me *more* than my own father. Lexi and I are going to live with you when Mom—"

"I get it," Monique cut me off, holding up her hand like she was warding off the word I hadn't said.

"What I meant is that you really are part of our family."

It was the closest I had ever seen Monique to tears. She patted my leg, realized it was awkward, and withdrew her hand quickly.

"I'm sorry," she said. "I should have told you about your changes, especially after the silver incident."

"What?"

"You had a reaction to the silver fork," she told me. "I had to give you some of my ointment to reverse its effects."

"So, that's what you put in my mouth."

"Yeah, and you would have been fine, but your mom insisted that you go to the emergency room."

"Can doctors tell I'm different?"

"Honestly, they're not looking for it, but you'll need to be more careful now. There are some irregularities in our blood and bones, especially when the moon's cycle ends. You don't want to be misdiagnosed with leukemia." She swung her feet lightly across my rug. "I thought you already knew about the way to prevent a cycle change. I found Moon's Bane in your mattress, and I hoped you had it covered."

"I didn't really change until last night," I told her.

"Really," she remarked. "Did you complete the Ritual?"

"Well, Loila's alive, so..."

"That poor girl."

"He hypnotized her," I said. "She doesn't remember anything."

Monique cocked her head and raised her eyebrows. "*He?*" she repeated. "You mean your dad?"

"I mean the person who abandoned his family, and doesn't feel the need to help his wife," I shot back.

"I guess you realize that your father was attacked by another werewolf," she began.

"That's what he said."

"I went after him," she revealed.

"Why didn't you kill him?" I quipped, and then I remembered her pronounced limp outweighed my father's injury. He had gotten the best of her.

"Hey!" Monique barked at me, and I heard something shift in the hall. "What's wrong with you? That's your dad!"

"He may have acted like it once, but he hasn't been around for six years," I justified. "Even longer, if I really think about it."

"You don't know what you're talking about. Why do you think *I'm* here?"

"You're my mom's best friend."

"I'm your *dad's* best friend."

The patterns on my rug danced while I took a couple of breaths. I had to admit, it made better sense after I thought about their personalities.

"He told me to stay here and not let anyone know that he was still alive," she continued.

"You *knew* he was alive," I squeaked out. I hated the way my voice sounded and the traitorous tears that threatened to spill. I felt completely betrayed.

Then it hit me. "*You* could have saved my mom, too."

"That's what this is really about, isn't it?" Monique sighed. "You think I should have been giving your mom doses of Moon's Bane since she found the lump in her breast."

"Why not?" I said defiantly.

"Because the risks are too high!" Monique hissed. "Do you want to see your mom snatched away and put in a cage because she's turned into a beast?"

"Why can't you give her little doses?" I argued.

"Because it will build in her system until she turns into something unnatural."

"Can't you even try?" I begged. The tears started, and I couldn't hold them back. "You may be his friend, but aren't you her friend, too?"

"Oh, honey," Monique spoke softly. "I love your mom. She is one of the kindest and most compassionate women I know. I want her to be here for you and Lexi. I want her to live."

She tried to hold my hand, but I jerked it away. She looked down at her feet and took a deep breath.

"Do you think it's what she'd want?" she asked me.

"I think she doesn't want to leave us," I pushed back.

"Your mom hasn't done chemotherapy," Monique pointed out. "She doesn't want an unorthodox cure."

"You don't know," I cried, heaving gulps of air that made me feel like I was drowning. Snot fell from my nose, and I wiped it uselessly. My mom was dying, and the people who could help her chose to stand by and watch. "She doesn't understand. We need to *make* her understand."

"Make her understand what?"

"How much I'll miss her!" I wailed. Monique rushed to embrace me, and I fell into her arms. I don't know how long I cried, but I must have fallen asleep between my sobs.

CHAPTER THIRTY-SIX

I didn't try to find my father again. Monique thought that it was best that Lexi and my mom believe that he was dead, so I kept the secret.

Her unseen killer slowly ebbed my mom's energy away. *I had the remedy for her pain, but how much more suffering would it cause if I gave it to her? Besides, I had become a monster on the outside. Did I really want my selfish actions to lead me in a direction that would upend my morality? Was I a monster on the inside, too?*

I watched Lexi for signs that she would turn. I thought it was too early for a gold glint to touch her irises, or a mound of random hair to appear, but I decided that I was going to be the one to tell her about the changes she was feeling before anyone else could screw it up.

Loila didn't seem to remember anything. She wore the emerald ring when she came to school the Monday after the banquet, and she didn't ask me about it. Maybe she knew that I had slipped it on her finger. Maybe she just liked the ring.

I thought I saw her looking at me strangely from time to time, but I shrugged it off. She probably wondered if I was going to ask her out or was surprised about the role I had played as her knight in shining armor. She would have been my girlfriend if I would have asked her, but it wasn't fair to pull her into my life when I had to stay silent about the changes I was going through. Look what had happened between my parents. It just wasn't worth it.

I was mad at Aiden until the school year ended. I tried to act like everything was okay around Loila and Tabitha, but they knew something was wrong. He apologized to me privately, but there was a void between us, an empty place where I had stored my trust in him over the nine years we had known each other.

After the way Aiden had used her to make Rowan jealous, Tabitha avoided him. Sadly, that meant that Loila and I rarely saw her, as we hung out with Aiden often.

Rowan messaged me almost every day. She'd send memes about werewolves and newspaper sightings. In August, she would be the one who warned me about the new threat. An old enemy had surfaced, and my father was missing.

———◇———

During the first full moon in June, I met my pack just outside of the North Carolina line. We changed fully, watching each other's bones break and readjust in the silver light. We chased after a deer, tracking its scent across miles of maples, evergreens, and free-flowing creeks. We charged and sniffed, circling the majestic buck that was out much later than most of the members of his species. I was the first to lunge and land on his back. I grabbed his throat with my mouth and snapped his neck. I tasted the salty blood as it covered my mouth, and I had never eaten anything better.

After we had changed back into our former selves, Aiden and I opened up to Dani and Bruce. I couldn't help the secrets I told. They leaked out of me naturally, until my soul was a puddle at their feet. I let them know about my mom and the fears I had about her death. Aiden confessed the sins of his mother and his resentment against his father. Dani and Bruce bared their secrets, and we promised not to tell, sealing our oaths with a pinky swear.

Before we left, I relieved myself in the woods, and Bruce met me away from the pack.

"You're right, ya know," he said. Drops of blood still dotted his chin. I motioned to them, and he wiped them with one of the baby wipes Dani had given each of us after we had bathed in the creek.

"You should be mad at your dad for not dosing your mom with Scorn," he clarified. "She has a better chance of living, and I know a couple of guys where I'm from that have taken it for years and they've never turned."

"The probability of her staying human isn't good," I countered, hating myself for playing the devil's advocate.

"If you say so," Bruce agreed amiably. "But I would rather try than just let my mom die. Once she's gone, that's it."

He raced back to the others and left me alone with my thoughts. When I rejoined them, Danni and Bruce were leaving.

Aiden and I ran down the mountain for a couple of miles. We paced ourselves. I had told my mom that I was spending the night with Aiden, and he was supposed to be staying with me, so no one was expecting us. We finally ended up in our cave.

"Are we going to stay here tonight?" I asked.

"We can go to my house," Aiden replied. "The staff won't call your mom."

"Whatever."

I had meant whatever he wanted to do, but Aiden took it another way.

"What's your problem, man?" he shouted. "I told you that I was sorry, but I only knew we were werewolves a couple of days before you. I was still processing it myself."

"I get it," I said, and shrugged my shoulders.

"What do you want me to say?" Aiden yelled. "Poor Razz! Everyone has to dance around you because your mom is about to die. I'm sorry you didn't know you were a werewolf, but guess what? I didn't know either! But instead of going through this together, you're just—"

"I'm sorry," I said, surprising both of us. My apology hung in the air.

"Okay," Aiden said, and that was it. Nothing more had to be said.

⚬

The day after my first kill, I walked into an empty house. I had been with Loila and Aiden at the cave, and Monique had taken my mom and Lexi to my mom's oncologist's office.

I grabbed a box of cheese snacks and headed to my room. The door handle rattled, and I doubled back to investigate the sound.

My mom peeked around the door, as if she expected me to be waiting for her. She was the color of milk, and her skin drooped forward in small folds. It was hot outside, and her perspiration was thick with disease. I dropped my snack and caught her before she fell. I practically dragged her to the couch and draped her across the fluffy cushions.

"Where's Monique and Lexi?" I admonished.

"I told them to go get ice cream," my mom said between breaths. "Lexi is having a terrible summer."

She made light of her condition, but I didn't respond to her joke. "What if I hadn't been here? You'd be on the floor!"

"Easy, Razzberry," she spoke. "I needed to talk to you, and I didn't want Lexi to eavesdrop."

I poured a ginger ale into a small cup and brought it to my mom. She accepted it gratefully, but she only took a few sips. I had hidden my cheese snacks in the highest kitchen cabinet. The smell of the open box made her gag.

I waited for her to reveal the reason she had sent Lexi and Monique away. Her time was short, and she knew the best way to use every second.

"You wanted to know where I was on the night your father died."

The room gathered the buzz of silence. I put pressure on my legs to keep them from shaking.

"I had gone to a lawyer to file for a divorce."

Her face crumbled, and she rolled onto my lap. Her shoulder bones cut into my skin as sobs shook her small frame. I didn't think my mom's disease would allow her such a strong physical reaction.

"I'm sorry," she wailed. "I know you wanted him to come back home, but I was scared."

I was starting to worry that her admission would cause her an unplanned trip to the hospital. She didn't know my father was alive, or that my feelings about him had changed, and I couldn't tell her. I felt like it was my duty to make her feel better.

"Hey, Mom," I soothed. "It's all good. It was a long time ago."

My mom hiccupped and gently lifted herself back onto the couch cushions. Her outburst had only made her face slightly pink, like she'd spent the morning in the sun.

"You aren't mad at me?"

"Why would I be mad at you? He left us, and you have every right to be happy." She turned her head thoughtfully. "Besides," I reasoned, "he's dead now, so you don't need a divorce."

"Razzberry, that's a terrible thing to say," she scolded, but she didn't have the energy to be truly upset. "Actually, I still feel like I'm married." She stole a glance at me and turned away quickly.

I don't know what I would have told her if Lexi and Monique hadn't barged through the door. I might have thought of something cute to spin off her words, but my voice was robbed from me when Lexi climbed into my lap with dried ice cream on her nose. I looked into my little sister's eyes and saw a golden glint flash like lightning across her irises.

CHAPTER THIRTY-SEVEN

My mom lay dying. Every breath she took shook in her chest.

After the full moon in June, the doctor assigned her to hospice care. Nurses brought her oxygen, changed her IV bag, and put liquid meals into bags that pumped straight into her intestines.

Food nauseated her. Lexi and I ate crackers and salad without dressing. Our mom could smell any other food on us, and it made her sick.

I carried the television into her room, and Lexi and I watched movies with her. She slept most of the time, and when she woke, she wasn't always conscious of my sister and me.

Monique stayed with us at night. She started out on the couch, but she always migrated to the chair beside my mom.

I laid at the foot of my mom's bed at night, unless my breathing was too much movement for her. On those nights, I'd slip onto the floor, falling asleep to the sound of her ragged breaths and waking when there was too much time between them.

Several times, I thought I saw a figure at my mom's window, bathed in moonlight. I wasn't scared, and I didn't try to alert anyone. The creatures of the night are only scary when you're not one of them.

Lexi was usually vivacious, but her personality muted. She drew pictures all day and put them around our mother's bed as if she were drawing a circle against death. She kept trying to sketch a picture of our mom, but she couldn't seem to get it right.

"Her hair isn't that dark!" she yelled at herself and collapsed into tears at the kitchen table.

I picked her up and walked her to the YMCA's pool to decompress. We came back quickly, though, afraid that we'd miss precious moments with our mom.

Our time with her was growing short, and the more I looked into the gasping face of the woman who gave me life, the more uncertain I was about the rationale behind Monique's and my father's reasons.

CHAPTER THIRTY-EIGHT

On a hot day in July, I sat on the end of my dying mother's bed. Her breathes weren't quite rattling, but her time was noticeably drawing to a close.

Lexi and I had wheeled her hospice bed to the edge of the room to watch part of a fireworks show from the corner of her window. To anyone else, it would have been a lame way to spend the holiday, but we stood there beside her, holding each other with every boom and burst of light.

Lexi fell asleep after the fireworks, and Monique stayed in the living room. It gave me some time with my mom during what could be her last burst of true consciousness.

"Can I ask you to do one more thing with me?" I asked.

My mom hesitated. She didn't want to deny my request, but she was limited by her illness.

"Don't worry," I said. "I only want to cheer the holiday with you."

My mom smiled at the mention of something unique to our family. "Should we wake Lexi?"

"No," I said quickly. "It would be better to let her sleep, and I want to share this moment with you."

My mom nodded her agreement, a light shining in her eyes where they had been dulled. She was excited about the opportunity to share something with me.

I slipped into the kitchen. My mom could only keep down sips of clear soda or water, so I poured a small amount of an uncaffeinated beverage for us in two glasses, spilling some on the counter in my haste. My mom could only drink a swallow at a time, but I hoped she'd sip on it through the night until it was gone.

I worried that the amber crystals would color the drink, but they swam around in a cyclone before they disappeared into the mixture. I fixed myself a glass of soda, dragged a paper towel across the spill, and popped it into the trash.

I'd lied to myself since the vial had landed in my possession. I may have thought I was the type of kid that would take a drug, but I couldn't convince myself to do it. The Scorn between my mattresses had never been meant for me, even though I'd envisioned myself taking it and tearing through anyone who tried to separate me from my sister. I may not have been able to get my mom the best medical care, but I could give her a better chance.

I carried my lie to my mom, and she accepted it with a smile. She thought she was honoring a heartfelt request that would bring a smile to my face when I pulled it from my memories. She had no idea how much thought had already been given to this moment.

She clinked my glass. "To you, Razzberry," she said, and lifted her glass to her lips.

In that moment, my mom drank the miracle that extended her life, and she swallowed the poison that made her an addict. I had thought my father and Monique were monsters for standing by and watching my mom die, but I had revealed my true nature in that moment. I was ruled by selfishness...and blood.

Razz's story will continue in Book Two of the Rasputin's Dynasty Series,
Rasputin's Dynasty,
and will conclude in Book Three,
Rasputin's Destiny.

Did You Like This Book?

If you enjoyed this story, would you please write a review on Amazon, Goodreads, and/or BookBub?

Something as simple as "I liked the story!" helps the author so much! Your feedback can make the book more visible to other readers, and it gives the author a reason to dance a jig when she sees your review!

You can sign up for Courtnee's newsletter, and you will receive exclusive bonus content, like cover reveals, sales, and news about upcoming releases.

Thank you for reading Rasputin's Scorn!

Acknowledgements

Stereling, you and your relationships have helped me form this book. You will find your stoicism and phrases within the pages. *Are you Razz?* No. You will always be more to me. You are stronger, faster, and more loyal to the people you choose. If you read the story, you will see the similarities between your ties with Legacee and Razz's and Lexi's interactions. Your devotion to Kinidy may have inspired some of the scenes between Razz and Loila, as your real-life friends-to-more romance continues to blissfully endure.

When I dedicated the book to Stereling and Legacee, I wrote that they are "rich kids." It's not only because of the song Legacee asked me to play every time I was in the car with them. They truly are rich in sibling love.

The songs on the playlist are linked with particular scenes and feelings. Metallica's "Don't Tread on Me" invokes the image of the ouroboros and the feeling of the factory as Razz makes a desperate decision. Twenty-One Pilot's "My Blood" has a dualistic meaning as the reader will gather from the final pages. It's one of my favorite songs, as the lyrics fit the way I feel about my children. I imagine Razz feels the same way about his mother and sister.

Tosha and Mama, thank you for your help! You each have provided me with invaluable feedback. Tosha is responsible for the design on my website, and she has always been my biggest fan. I released this book on her birthday because she told me it was one of her favorites. I'm so glad I can share stories with my mama, especially since she devours books like a whale swallows krill! No one will ever read a word of my work without it having passed across the eyes of these two ladies first!

My younger children are absolutely amazing, too! The first reason I write is to make my children proud of me. I hope I have had a respectable journey, and I've left behind a wonderful legacy!

Taylor Dawn, with Sweet15 Designs LLC, designed the eye-catching cover. She is truly talented, and I appreciate her work ethic and the compassion I see behind the decisions she makes involving her patrons.

My Book Bindings Review Team is amazing! I love the conversations I share with the members as they read my work. Thank you for your thought-provoking reviews!

I appreciate the TATTERED PAGES and Tina Hogan Grant's Read More Books Facebook pages for their support and encouragement! Readers and authors are comfortable and approachable on both sites. In fact, Tina Hogan Grant has helped me considerably in the publishing process, and I am thankful for her significant advice.

I love libraries! I'll provide a special deal to any library that reaches out to me about a copy of my book. I nurtured my fondness of words in a bank vault that had been converted into a children's reading nook, and I believe libraries, like my local library, Unicoi County Public Library, should thrive!

Thank you, readers! I value each and every one of you, and I appreciate the time you take to step into the worlds I create!

Allison's Cabbage Steak

Prep Time: 5 minutes
Bake time: 20 minutes
Total Time: 25 minutes
Yield: four cabbage steaks

Ingredients

- One green cabbage
- Four tablespoons of olive oil
- Two tablespoons of garlic salt
- a dash of paprika (to individual taste)
- red pepper flakes (optional for added heat)

Procedure

1. Wash the cabbage and cut the stem off the head. Cut the cabbage in half and cut the halves in half. Depending on the size of your cabbage, the process should leave you with four slices of cabbage that are no more than one inch thick.
2. Place the cabbage slices on a cooking sheet. Allow some space between the slices for more even cooking.
3. Brush the cabbage slices with olive oil, coating them well on all exposed sides.
4. Add garlic salt, paprika, and red pepper flakes
5. Bake at 400 degrees for twenty minutes, or until the leaves of the cabbage are brown and the center is tender. Cooking times may vary due to oven differences.
6. Allow the cabbage steaks to cool, but serve them warm and enjoy!

About the Author

Courtnee Turner Hoyle, author of the award-winning My Brother's Keeper, lives in Northeast Tennessee with her children and husband. She graduated with two undergraduate degrees and a Master of Arts in Teaching from East Tennessee State University. In addition to her published novels, Courtnee has written several short stories that have been anthologized. Courtnee enjoys reading, writing, and any reasonable music. She spends her days in comfortable chaos, avoiding sweet tea, chocolate, and unannounced visitors. Follow her on Instagram @pale_woods_mysteries and visit her website: www.courtneeturnerhoyle.com

More of Courtnee's Titles

Coming in October 2022!

Cascade
A Prequel to the Under Archard's Spell Series
By Courtnee Turner Hoyle

Cascade is content living in Gallow's Cove with her blended unicorn/mermaid family and dodging the advances of the new boy at school. She has memories of her time in Marilla, the mermaid capital city, but she hasn't returned since she fled with her mother and sisters and rejoined her father on the shore.

Mysterious earthquakes start to shake away her picture of her perfect life, as her mother is kidnapped during a meal with the mermaid king and the rest of her family is attacked. When Cascade is poisoned after her first kiss, she realizes that the horrors her family had tried to escape in the water have found their way onto the land. What's more, a powerful mermaid usurper is assassinating any creature who doesn't comply with his rule. Cascade, her family, and a group of rebels race to the only place rumored to have a magician who can help them. But can the fledgling magician aid the mere thousands of supernatural beings left after the usurper's mass slaughter? And if so, what price will Cascade, her family, and the other creatures have to pay?

More of Courtnee's Titles

Available Now!

Pale Woods Mystery Series, Book One

My Brother's Keeper
Courtnee Turner Hoyle

Seventeen-year-old Jerrod Miller has struggled with the guilt of his actions for an event that took place almost a year ago. His friends have abandoned him, his family ignores him, and he lost his best friend. To make matters worse, he was unable to access records that may have revealed his father's whereabouts. His sister, Ella, guides Jerrod as he tries to learn and accept secrets his family has tried to hide. However, a sinister spirit may be influencing Ella's actions, and it has an agenda of its own.

Sold on Amazon and on Courtnee's website!

More of Courtnee's Titles

Coming in August 2022!

PALE WOODS PARANORMAL SUSPENSE SERIES

SOLOMON'S TEARS
Courtnee Turner Hoyle

Are the ghosts in her house or in her mind?

Ketron Gouge is puzzled when she feels like one of her children is missing. A quick check calms her panicked mind, but the uncomfortable thought continues to concern her.

Ketron and her husband, Marvin, bought a home they hoped would be perfect for their growing family. Soon, however, Marvin develops a drinking problem and Ketron becomes more anxious about the mysterious shadows and disembodied crying in the house. Most of her five children seem to be conscious of the uncanny events, giving credence to Ketron's worries, but her best friend and therapist think it may be a product of her overstressed mind.

Ghosts from her past and memories of her childhood tumble to the surface, reminding her of her mentally unstable mother, and she begins to wonder if there's truth to the nagging idea that someone is missing. And when she begins seeing things in her house, she thinks it may be time to accept an inescapable truth.

Bibliography

Lil Wayne (featuring Drake). Dwayne Carter, Jr. "Right Above It"
I Am Not a Human Being, Lil Wayne, 2010, Track 7

New Medicine. Kevin Kadish and Jake Scherer. "Rich Kids"
Race You to the Bottom, Atlantic Records, 2010, Track 2

Pinkfong. "Baby Shark" *Pinkfong Animal Songs*, Pinkfong, 2018, Track 7

Werner, Thomas. "The Chicken Dance" *Musicnotes*. Retrieved 22 April, 2019

Ylvis. Vegard Ylvisåker Bård Ylvisåker "What Does the Fox Say?"
The Fox, Urheim Records, 2013, Track 1